Double Life

Double Life

Zari

www.urbanbooks.net

Urban Books, LLC
300 Farmingdale Road, N.Y.-Route 109
Farmingdale, NY 11735

ISBN 13: 978-1-64556-554-3
EBOOK ISBN: 978-1-64556-576-5

First Trade Paperback Printing January 2024
Printed in the United States of America

10 9 8 7 6 5 4 3 2 1

Distributed by Kensington Publishing Corp.
Submit Orders to:
Customer Service
400 Hahn Road
Westminster, MD 21157-4627
Phone: 1-800-733-3000
Fax: 1-800-659-2436

Chapter One

For real estate agent and investor Alexis Fox, the day was finally over. That morning, she had two clients to show properties, a final walk-through with a buying client, and then she would rush back to her office to attend closings with clients to sign the sales contract and become the new owner of the property.

Later that evening, Alexis had a meeting with Imani Mosley to present their final offer for the Plaza Hotel and Suites. They met when Imani's family moved to Jacksonville from Miami, and she sold them a six-bedroom home in Ponte Vedra Beach, a suburb of Jacksonville. Alexis didn't know it at the time, but the Mosley family business was guns and drugs. The two enterprising young women became fast friends and eventually business partners. Their first investment together was The Park at Atlantic Beach, a multiunit property that they were in the process of converting into condominiums.

The next day, dressed in a gray and black two-tone Alexander McQueen Prince of Wales virgin wool suit and Gucci Sylvie chain heel sandals, Alexis got in her Avalon Hybrid and went to put in her work for another long day. After a stop at the Starbucks drive-through for a spinach, feta, and egg white wrap and grande cappuccino, she was in the office at seven thirty that morning.

Her day began with a review of her schedule for the day, and then she responded to the emails that she had received the day before. Once that was done, a good bit of her morning was spent on lead generation, using the new real estate CRM software that she installed, which allowed Alexis to manage her leads. With that tool, she would know where her clients stood in the sales cycle so she could use the email marketing function to send them the right message about the right property at the right time. And then she spent some time doing research on mymls.com, a multiple listing service, to prepare to show the Andersons properties that afternoon.

Alexis was out of the office by nine thirty to attend a home inspection at ten to evaluate a property that she was selling from a structural and safety standpoint. Checking the foundation, the roof, the plumbing, and the electrical and HVAC systems took up the rest of the morning, and then it was off to make a listing presentation at one that afternoon.

"I know that you are going to absolutely love this house. It has new doors, bay granite counters, an upgraded kitchen, and a saltwater pool. You are absolutely going to love this space," Alexis said as she unlocked the door to a stunning home in Pablo Bay. "This five-bedroom, four-bathroom home has been meticulously cared for and has plenty of upgrades."

She stepped through the main public area and made a sweeping gesture with her hand. "Notice how the fifteen-foot ceiling creates a wide-open space while looking over the saltwater pool and lake to the rear of the property," Alexis said as she walked her prospective buyers into the kitchen. "The kitchen is bright, spacious, and well-lit. All of the appliances have been upgraded, and then there are the granite counters," she said, running her hand along the counter. "The home features three suites with an owner's suite downstairs, and the upstairs bonus room as a third suite with a balcony attached."

She closed out her day showing the Andersons more properties, and then it was back to the office to make notes on the day and review the next day's schedule. Alexis was out of the office to meet the contractor at The Park at Atlantic Beach. She called Imani on the way.

"I'm not going to be able to make our strategy session, Imani. It's been a crazy day."

"No problem. I was going to call and tell you that I was tied up with something too," Imani said.

"But we are still on for tonight, right?"

"Most definitely."

"Great."

"See you tonight," Imani said and ended the call.

While the contractor inspected the units and wrote up price quotes, Alexis made calls. Therefore, when she was getting ready to leave, it was almost seven o'clock, and she was running late picking up Imani for their eight o'clock meeting. When she got there, Alexis found that Imani was running a little behind too, so it gave her a chance to talk briefly with Hareem, Imani's younger brother, and meet his daughter, Omeika. Once Imani was ready, they were on their way to make their presentation. After their offer for the Plaza Hotel and Suites was accepted, Alexis took Imani back to her house, and then she went home.

As soon as she got home, she kicked out of her Gucci sandals, got out of her suit, ran a hot bath, and sank into it with a glass of wine. While she soaked, Alexis asked herself the question that she had been asking herself for weeks.

"How much longer can I keep this up?"

Since she didn't have an answer, she took another sip of wine and closed her eyes. Alexis had been out late the night before and didn't get home until almost four in the morning. After a few hours of sleep, she was back up to start another day. That was how it had been lately, and the way things were going, it didn't seem like that was going to change anytime soon.

When the water began to get cold, she got out, dried herself, and laid out her clothes for the night. Alexis began with an Alice + Olivia Avelina vegan leather wide-leg jumpsuit, and Devonte embroidered leather moto jacket, with Giuseppe Zanotti mock-croc zip combat booties, and then she selected her jewelry. Alexis put on a pair of limited-edition Syna abalone drop earrings, and she looked in the mirror.

She complemented the outfit with a Nikos Koulis Oui eighteen-karat white gold teardrop enamel pendant necklace with diamonds, and an eighteen-karat white gold three-row diamond coil bracelet. Alexis chose an eternity band diamond ring, a three-stone diamond ring for her left hand, a black and onyx diamond ring because it matched her outfit, and a crossover wide diamond ring because it was her favorite.

When she was dressed, she grabbed her black Chloe Serpui Laila floral straw wooden top-handle bag, put on a pair of oversized round acetate light-adaptive sunglasses, got in her Jaguar F-Type coupe, and headed out for the night. When she arrived at her destination, she parked and walked to the door and rang the bell. After a while, Cameron opened the door.

"What's up, Diamond? Come on in."

For the past ten years, Alexis Fox had been living a double life. She was a successful real estate agent and investor by day, and by night she was the drug queen pin known in the streets as Diamond.

"Where are they?"

"In the back," Cameron said and led the way to the bedrooms in the house. When they got to the first room, LaLa Hogan was standing at the door with his nine in his hand. He opened the door, and Alexis looked in. Angela

Hampton, the wife of Marques Hampton, was in the room, and she was gagged and tied to the bed.

"Why is she tied up?"

"She's a wildcat. It took three of us to get her under control," Cameron informed, and Alexis shook her head. She walked into the room.

"Take the gag out of her mouth."

Once Cameron had removed the gag, Alexis stepped to the bed.

"Hello, Angela."

"Hey, Diamond," she said in a quivering voice.

"You wanna be alive in the morning?" Alexis took out her gun and pointed it at Angela. "Or should I just shoot you now?"

Angela nodded her head quickly. "I wanna be alive."

"Good. I'm gonna have him cut you loose, okay?" Angela nodded, and Alexis lowered her weapon. "When he does, I need you to be cool and be quiet while I talk to your man. Do you think you can do that for me?"

"Yes." Angela nodded. "I can do that. But let me explain."

"What did I just say?" Alexis asked, returning the gun to her head. "I said for you to be quiet, right?" Angela nodded her head. "So, what does that mean?"

"It means don't say nothing."

"Right." Once again, Alexis lowered her weapon. "You'll have plenty of time to explain when I come back."

Alexis turned and left the room with Cameron. "Leave the door open, LaLa," she told him as she passed. She looked back at Angela. "If she makes a sound or moves off that bed, kill her. Understand?"

"Got it," LaLa said as Alexis went to the next room.

Marques Hampton was seated on the bed, and three of her men—Henderson, D'shaun, and Jarell—were armed and in the room with him.

"Give me a chance to explain," Marques said as soon as Alexis appeared in the doorway.

"Shut up!" She looked at her men. "Why isn't he tied up?" she asked the second she saw him.

"He wasn't no problem like Angela," D'shaun said to her as she walked into the room.

She looked around the room. "Bring him in the living room, tie him up, gag him, and then tie him to a chair."

"Please, Diamond, let me explain," Marques said as Henderson, D'shaun, and Jarell moved toward him.

Alexis stepped toward him quickly and put her gun to his head. "Shut the fuck up. Time for you to talk to me is over." Henderson put the gag in his mouth. "You'll have plenty of time to explain yourself later," she said before moving her gun away from his head and walking out of the room.

Alexis went into the living room and sat down in Marques's infinite reclining chair and made herself comfortable while her men brought Marques out and tied him to a chair. Once he was tied securely, she nodded her head. D'shaun stepped in front of Marques, and the beating began. He stood in front of Marques, throwing hard punches to his head, shoulders, and stomach.

When he stopped to catch his breath, Alexis said, "Henderson," and he took over the brutal beating until his hands hurt. At that point, Alexis ordered Jarell to take over, and he took his turn.

Marques's face was a bloody and twisted mess when Alexis got up and went into the bathroom. She stopped up the drain in Angela and Marques's brand new seventy-one-inch modern acrylic Jacuzzi tub and turned on the water. When it was full, she went back into the living room where D'shaun had resumed the beating.

"Bring him."

Alexis turned around and went back to the bathroom. Jarell and D'shaun grabbed Marques out of the chair, and since he wasn't walking that well, they dragged him into the bathroom. When they got in the bathroom and Jarell saw the tub filled with water, he smiled and wasted no time getting Marques to the tub and forcing his face underwater. He fought and struggled as Jarell held his head underwater until Alexis said to pull him up. Marques spit out water and tried to catch his breath.

"Again," Alexis ordered.

Jarell gladly held Marques's head underwater until Alexis nodded her head.

"Pull him up and take the gag out of his mouth."

Jarell complied with her request, and once the gag was out, Marques inhaled deeply and tried to catch his breath.

"I'm sorry, Diamond," he said to her as she walked out of the bathroom.

"Bring him."

She went back into the living room, sat down in the recliner, and waited for them to bring Marques out. When her men let him go, his beaten body fell to the floor.

"Pick him up and hold him."

Once again, her men complied with her request.

"Where's my money?"

"In the safe."

"Does Angela know the combination?"

Marques nodded quickly. "Yes."

"Where's my dope?"

"In the streets."

"Does Angela know who has it?"

Marques nodded quickly. "Yes."

Alexis got up and stood in front of him. "Good. You're still gonna die."

Alexis raised her gun and shot Marques once in the head. When his body fell to the ground, she stood over him and shot him twice more in the chest. She handed Cameron her gun.

"Get rid of it," she said and returned to the bedroom where Angela was waiting. She stood in the doorway.

"Get up and get my money from the safe."

"Okay." Angela got up and started for the door. "I'm sorry, Diamond. I swear I didn't know what Marques was doing until yesterday, and that's when I called you."

While she opened the safe, Angela explained how Marques had staged a robbery with Slaughter. Their plan was for Angela to come home and find the front door kicked in. When she went into the house, she would find him and Slaughter tied up on the floor with the dope and the money gone.

"Where's Slaughter?" Alexis asked once she saw the money in the safe.

"I don't know. I swear, Diamond, I don't know where he is," Angela said, scared for her life but hoping that Diamond meant what she said about her being alive in the morning.

"I believe you, Angela. And I'm sure that no shit like this is ever gonna happen again," Alexis said and walked toward the door. "If anything like this ever happens again, I will make you wish that I had killed you tonight."

Chapter Two

Ten Years Earlier

"South Jacksonville Realty, my name is Alexis Fox. How can I help you today?"

"Good morning, Ms. Fox. My name is Albert Bell," he said in a deep and sexy voice that made her sit up and pay attention. "I was referred to you by Denise Evans. You sold her a house recently, and she said that you took good care of her."

"Yes." Alexis quickly accessed her information. "I was able to show Denise a four-bedroom home on Spoonbills Street that she is very happy with."

"It's a beautiful house."

"It really is," Alexis said as she scrolled through images of the property. "Tell me how I can help you, Mr. Bell."

"I'm interested in buying a house."

"I would be more than happy to show you some properties. How soon are you looking to get started?"

"I was hoping to start looking right away."

"Awesome. Why don't we do this—are you free tomorrow?"

"All day."

"Are you familiar with the Panera Bread on San Jose Boulevard?"

"No, but I am sure I can find it."

"Is that location good for you?"

"Yeah, sure."

"Great. Why don't we meet there tomorrow? What time is good for you?"

"I'm free all day, so whatever is good for you."

"Say, eleven o'clock?"

"That works for me."

"Fantastic!" Alexis said enthusiastically. "I will see you tomorrow morning at the Panera Bread on San Jose Boulevard at eleven o'clock."

"I'll see you then."

"I am looking forward to meeting you. Enjoy the rest of your day," she said and hung up the phone.

Alexis sat back in her chair, excited about the call she had just ended. Another appointment to show a property was a good thing for the new agent. Not only that, but she was also intrigued by the sound of Mr. Bell's voice.

Alexis had graduated from Florida State University with a degree in management information systems and a master of science in finance from Florida International University, but when it came time to get a job after graduation, she chose to get into the real estate business because the potential for earning large commissions was greater than the industry starting salary for the entry-level IT positions that she'd been offered.

In the four months that she had been a licensed agent, Alexis had sold three properties. She was lucky on her first sale. It was a walk-in on her third day. He had come to see the agency's golden girl, Jennifer Davenport, but she resigned the Friday before, and Alexis was the only one in the office when he came in. After three weeks of her showing him houses, her first client settled on a $900,000 five-bedroom home on Water Chase Way East. The following month she sold two $500,000 homes: one on Spoonbills Street and the other on Falcon Crest Drive.

If she could close this sale, it would make for another great month for her, and so far, Alexis had been doing all right. The average real estate sales salary for a new associate was somewhere around $65,000, but at the pace she was selling, Alexis saw herself making well over $100,000 that year.

The following morning, Alexis got up and began what was becoming her morning routine. Alexis checked for new listings that would fit her client's criteria, and then she got up and went to her closet to select something to wear for her appointment with sexy-talking Albert Bell. She chose an ivory and black two-tone lace crepe sheath dress by Tadashi Shoji and a pair of Badgley Mischka Tierra ankle-bracelet pumps, and then she got in the shower.

Once she was dressed, she was going to head for the Panera Bread on San Jose Boulevard, but she realized that she needed to stop at the office first. When she got to the office, Alexis did what she needed to do, and then she was on her way out the door. Cynthia Miles, the new office manager, was just arriving for the day. She was the daughter of Alexander and Clairice Miles, who owned the firm. South Jacksonville Realty was the largest black-owned-and-operated real estate firm in North Florida. They were friends until Cynthia's mother began heaping praises on Alexis when she began to outsell her. Since Cynthia was lazy and liked to fuck more than sell houses, her mother's intention was to spark her daughter's competitive nature. When that didn't work, Clairice recently promoted her to the office manager position.

"Good morning, Cynthia," Alexis said brightly as she passed her on the way out the door.

"Hey," she said quietly without making eye contact and kept it moving.

"I know you're not just getting here. How do you expect to run this office if you can't get here on time?" Alexis heard Clairice shout when she saw her daughter come in.

She laughed to herself and kept it moving to her Honda Accord that she was thinking seriously about trading. If she was going to chauffeur potential clients around to show them properties, she needed to get a car that said, "I'm a successful agent." She started her car and drove away thinking that her car said, "I'm just getting by," and that was not the image that she needed to portray.

When Alexis arrived at Panera, she parked and went inside to wait. She ordered a cup of cafe-blend dark roast coffee, and since she hadn't eaten that morning and she was hungry, she thought about ordering her favorite toasted steak and white cheddar sandwich, but having a mouthful of steak and white cheddar when the client arrived would not be a good look. So, Alexis got her coffee and found a seat. She was sipping coffee and looking out the window when a silver late-model Mercedes-Benz A-Class rolled into the parking lot.

"I need something like that," she said and picked up her phone to price it as she caught a glimpse of the man who got out. "'Clean lines, LED lighting, and an aggressive stance aim for admiring eyes. An ultramodern, premium cabin can captivate you for years to come,'" Alexis was reading from the website when she noticed that he was standing there.

"Ms. Fox?"

That voice, Alexis thought as a chill washed over her. "Yes." She looked up and saw Albert Bell, and her heart all but stopped beating. "Mr. Bell?"

"Yes."

"Thank you for meeting me," Alexis said to the dark-skinned, six-foot-three-inch man. He was wearing a camel T-shirt that showed off his bulging biceps with black slim-fit jeans that took her breath away. "Please sit down."

"Thank you," he said while smiling at Alexis as he sat down across from her. "Denise described you perfectly."

"Did she?"

"She did. She said that you are hands down one of the most beautiful women she'd ever seen in person."

"That was so nice of her to say."

"It's true. You are beautiful," he said, and it caused Alexis to smile shyly. "I started to call you and cancel because I had something else to do, but when I got here and I saw you through the window when I parked, I knew that it was you. She was right. You are beautiful."

"Thank you, Mr. Bell," she said, thinking that he was a very handsome man, one Alexis wouldn't mind getting to know, but this was business. She was there to sell him a house. Once she closed the sale, then she would see where things went from there.

"You can call me Bells. Everybody else does."

"Alexis," she said with her hand extended. When he shook her hand, Alexis felt chills running up and down her spine.

"It's a pleasure to meet you, Alexis," Bells said, holding her hand and staring into her eyes.

Although neither of them knew it, in that second, they had fallen in love with one another.

"Pleasure to meet you too." She paused until he let go of her hand. "Can I get you something? Coffee or something to eat?"

"Just coffee."

Alexis started to get up. "How do you take it?"

"Black." Bells stood up. "But you relax. I'll go get it."

Wow, a gentleman. "Okay."

"Do you want anything?"

Alexis pointed to her cup. "I'm fine, thank you."

"I'll be right back," he said and walked away.

Alexis watched him as he walked away from the table. Yes, he was fine, but Albert Bell was a man in his early twenties. To this point, her clients had been over 40, so she hoped that he was serious about buying a house and not wasting her time. She had given her card to a younger man once before, and all he did was waste her time trying to arrange a date with her. After two weeks of that, she had to cut him loose and found a real buying client, and that was when she sold her second house.

As Bells came back with his coffee, Alexis looked him up and down and came to the conclusion that if he asked her out, she would accept whether he bought a house or not. To her, he was just that fine.

"The reason I wanted to meet," Alexis began, "was so we would have an opportunity to talk and I can get an idea of what you're looking for in a home."

"I was thinking about a house like the one you sold Denise."

Yes! Alexis said to herself, because she had sold Denise a $500,000 home. She opened her laptop, and once she entered the search criteria, she got up and moved to sit next to him in the booth, and once again, Alexis felt chills running up and down her spine. The two sat shoulder to shoulder and looked at pictures of properties.

"That one is nearby. You wanna take a look at it?"

"Sure, why not?"

"Awesome," Alexis said and closed her laptop and committed herself to selling him a property that day.

When they walked out of Panera together, each sneaking glances at the other, she pointed to her car. "Why don't you ride with me?"

He moved a little closer to her as they walked, and her body trembled unconsciously. "Why don't you ride with me?" Bells said and unlocked the Mercedes-Benz A-Class that she was admiring. "I insist."

"Okay," she said and walked alongside him. He opened the door for her to get in. "Thank you."

When he got in, Alexis gave him the address to the property. Bells entered it into the vehicle's navigation system, and they set out. They looked at two houses, and at the end of the day, he invited her to have dinner with him, and Alexis accepted.

Dinner that night turned into dinner and cocktails at Bahama Breeze later that evening and a promise to meet to look at more houses the following day. It allowed them the opportunity to become more familiar with one another, talking and laughing. He was charming and funny, and Alexis found herself enjoying the witty banter that they were exchanging.

Their time together that day raised a huge red flag for her. First off, Bells had two cell phones that rang constantly. By the end of the day, Alexis had lost count of how many times he said, "Excuse me. I gotta take this."

What it told her was that Albert Bell, aka Bells, was a drug dealer, and now Alexis had to think about a couple of things. The question was, did she want to spend time house hunting with him? It may prove to be a waste of her time. She had uncles, aunts, and a few cousins serving time in prisons around the state on drug offenses. It wasn't as if she was unfamiliar with the drug life, but it was a life that she was trying to get away from.

Alexis got in bed that night thinking that she liked him. They had just spent a wonderful day together. She wanted to see him again, so that settled that. Therefore, when he called the next morning wanting to look at houses, she said, "Meet me at Panera at ten."

Chapter Three

At ten o'clock, Alexis watched Bells's Mercedes-Benz roll into the parking lot at Panera. She always made it a practice of arriving fifteen minutes before an appointment, so she was there at nine forty-five. The night before, Alexis tossed and turned for hours before she was able to drift off to sleep. For more reasons than one, Bells had captured her mind and wouldn't let her get comfortable in bed.

There was only one question, but it led down two separate and very distinct paths. She didn't necessarily want to stereotype him, but Alexis had come to the conclusion that Albert "You Can Call Me Bells" Bell was a drug dealer. It was written all over his face, his speech, his mannerisms. It all said, "I'm a drug dealer." And if that were the case, how much time did she want to invest in him? And that went for her personal feelings as well as business.

"Good morning, Alexis."

"Good morning, Mr. Bell."

That morning, he was wearing a Polo camouflage crewneck T-shirt and drawstring shorts that showed off his bulging biceps and muscular thighs, and he was wearing them well.

"Bells. Please, call me Bells. When you say Mr. Bell, I start looking around for my daddy."

Alexis let out a little laugh. "Okay, Bells it is. Please have a seat."

"Thank you." Bells sat down next to her, and Alexis felt that chill wash over her again. "How are you this morning?"

"I'm doing great today. What about you? How are you this morning?"

"Great. Ready to look at some houses."

"Great!" Alexis opened her laptop. "I've got some really nice places that I want to show you today."

"Cool," he said excitedly. "But before we do that, you think we could get a little something-something to eat? I'm starving."

"Not a problem."

While the pair sat shoulder to shoulder and ate a chipotle chicken, scrambled egg, and avocado sandwich on ciabatta and a bacon, scrambled egg, and cheese on brioche sandwich and sipped coffee, Alexis showed him a variety of properties, and they settled on three that he wanted to look at that day.

"Let's find you a house," Alexis said enthusiastically and stood up.

Bells stood up and looked at Alexis from head to toe. "You look very nice in that," he said, focusing on the way her legs looked in the Etney Dickey plaid blazer and matching Inara tweed shorts and Foley suede strappy sandals, all by Veronica Beard, that she was wearing that day.

"Thank you," she said and debated whether to compliment him on his outfit and how good he looked in it.

When they walked out of Panera, Bells smiled as they got closer to his car. "Can you catch?"

"Not really. Why?"

"You know where we're going. You drive." He tossed the keys to the car to Alexis. She was caught off guard, but she caught them. "Thought you couldn't catch."

"Sometimes I get lucky and just hold out my hand. It was luck, believe me."

The first house that they looked at was a fabulous home that was located on a quiet street in close proximity to downtown Jacksonville.

"It has a private backyard on approximately half an acre of land," she said as they got out of the car and walked toward the house. She unlocked the lockbox, got the key, and opened the door. "This property has it all. High ceilings and exquisite architectural details, hardwood floors, vaulted ceilings, extensive custom wall molding, and floor-to-ceiling fireplaces." They went into the kitchen. "The gourmet kitchen features lovely bar seating, beautiful granite countertops, and loads of custom cabinetry."

"I'm not much of a cook, so I'll be spending very little time in here."

"What do you do, Mr. Bell?"

"I'm in sales. I like the way the morning sun fills this room," he said, quickly changing the subject as they left the kitchen and went upstairs.

"The second floor has three bedrooms and a spacious bath with a walk-in shower."

Despite being impressed by the new roof, fresh exterior and interior paint, new carpet in the bedrooms, the landscaping, and the two-car garage with a long driveway and plenty of off-street parking, Bells passed on that house, so it was on to the next property that Alexis had selected for him to look at that day. The drive there gave them more time to talk and get acquainted, and they found that they had quite a bit in common. They both considered themselves to be romantics and enjoyed being romanced.

"I know it's hard to believe, but yes, I am a hopeless romantic," he said.

To which Alexis thought, *I'll be very interested to see just how romantic you can be.*

"So am I," she said instead.

Although neither of them was in one, they both admitted that they liked being in a relationship. They were both driven by the things that they felt passionate about, and each one talked about the importance of alone time.

"I appreciate the little things. Say something nice to me, meaningful touches—that's the kind of thing that my heart desires more than elaborate gestures," Alexis said.

"I'll have to keep that in mind."

I'll be very interested to see, Alexis thought but didn't comment on it as they arrived at the next house.

"This house is Energy Star certified," she said as they approached the two-story, four-bedroom, three-bathroom house with a loft and two-car garage. "The oversized primary suite offers a separate spacious walk-in closet as well as a vanity with dual sinks in the primary bath. The backyard is large enough to add a pool, it backs up to woods, and it is located in a cul-de-sac."

"It's nice, but what else you got?" Bells said. Alexis was starting to get a little discouraged and wondered if she was wasting her time trying to sell him a house.

"I have one more property that I want to show you today," she said when they got back in the car. "It's a two-story, four-bedroom, three-bathroom house, and it's Energy Star certified as well." She started the car, and Bells made himself comfortable.

"Well, let's check it out. This one may be it," he said.

They went to look at the house, but once again Bells passed on it.

It was after five that afternoon when a disappointed Alexis parked the Benz next to her Honda. She was disappointed that Bells didn't seem all that excited about anything that she had showed him, but she was very encouraged about Bells and the possibilities.

"Sorry we couldn't find your perfect house today."

"That's all right. I had a nice time hanging out with you today."

"I enjoyed you too."

"And we'll find a house."

"And it will be perfect."

"That's right."

"If you're free tomorrow, there are some more places I can show you."

"Sounds good," he said, and then an uncomfortable silence crept in between them because it was time for them to separate and neither one was ready to do that. "What are you getting ready to do?"

"Going back to the office. I still have some prospecting and appointment setting that I need to do. And I like to spend that time evaluating what I accomplished today and what my goals are for tomorrow."

"A very wise practice." He smiled, and Alexis felt herself get a little wet. "But let me make a suggestion."

"What's that?"

"We haven't eaten since breakfast, and I don't know about you, but I'm hungry."

"I am too. I was gonna hit the drive-through at Hardee's and grab a burger on the way to the office."

Bells frowned and shook his head. "No, no, no. We not having that. I mean, you can have a burger if you want to, but I suggest that we go someplace nice, sit down, enjoy a nice dinner, and have a fascinating conversation. What do you say to that?"

"I say where do you want to eat?"

"And I say that you're driving."

"Okay." Alexis started the Benz. "There's a place that I've been dying to try."

"What's that?"

"It's called the Black Sheep Restaurant. It's a roof-top lounge and restaurant overlooking downtown Jacksonville, the Riverside area, and the St. Johns River. They tell me the view is awesome and I'll love it!"

"I'm down for that."

After a meal of short ribs with stewed black-eyed peas and chicken ballotine, dirty rice, spoonbread, and an amazing conversation, the pair left the Black Sheep Restaurant and got in the car. Once again, an uncomfortable silence crept in between the otherwise chatty couple until Bells leaned closer and broke the ice.

"I enjoyed the day."

"I did too."

Bells paused for a second and shifted in his seat. "Suppose I were to say that I wanted to take you to the best hotel in the city so I could make love to you. What would you say?"

The question may have caught her off guard, but since she had been fantasizing about him making love to her all day, Alexis had an answer.

"I wouldn't say anything." She started the car. "I would just start the car and drive to the best hotel in the city so you could make love to me."

After that, not another word passed between them as Alexis drove to the Riverfront Hyatt Regency in downtown Jacksonville, and Bells checked them into one of the hotel's St. Johns suites. As soon as they were in the suite and closed the door, his lips captured hers, and his hands unbuttoned her shorts. She quickly wiggled out of them, and he began peeling down her wet panties as their lips met again.

Alexis began unbuckling his pants, and he stepped out of them quickly. Cradling her face in his big hands, he kissed her hard and hungrily. She kissed him back. His lips and his kisses were hot and demanding, and

Alexis got caught up in the passion. The feeling of his skin against hers and his hands caressing her body was intense. No man had ever touched her that way, and no man had ever made her feel the things he was making her feel.

Bells explored the inside of her mouth with slow and sensual strokes, licking and tasting her until she moaned with pleasure, making her grind, writhing against him. She felt the river flowing freely between her thighs, and she moved faster. He took his time undressing Alexis, deliberately removing each piece and pausing in between. Once they were naked, he broke their embrace and took a step back to admire her.

"Damn," he said in a voice barely above a whisper, and his lips cupped hers again.

Bells took Alexis by the hand, and they rushed into the bedroom in the suite. He laid her out on the bed, and with the moist heat of his mouth, Bells licked and sucked her nipples in ways that made her entire body feel like it would melt under his touch.

Bells pushed her legs back toward her chest, and Alexis spread her legs wide to accommodate him. As his circling finger rubbed her engorged clit, it made her feel as if she would explode. Alexis wanted him so badly that she could barely think straight. Her lips opened, and Alexis took his tongue deep into her mouth. She enjoyed the sensation of their tongues dancing and wrestling for dominance.

"I want to feel you inside me," Alexis whispered.

Bells put a condom on and rubbed the head of his dick up and down her wet lips before he entered her in one long, hard thrust. She was just that wet for him. Alexis wrapped her arms around his neck and her legs around his waist, and Bells began pumping in and out, working her slowly and thoroughly, giving her inch by delicious inch, leisurely and deeply. The energy that each felt built to a crescendo, and it sent waves through Alexis that she felt all over her body.

Bells raised his head. He was staring at her like she was the most precious thing in the world to him. Alexis gazed into his eyes. "What are you doing to me?" she asked, mesmerized by the love they were making.

She closed her eyes, took deep breaths, and held on tight as her body shuddered to pieces in sheer ecstasy. Bells's pace was slow and constant as he slid in and out of her, wanting to feel every sensation that her warmth had to offer. She kissed his neck and chest, loving the way he felt inside her. Alexis's body was on fire and burning with a kind of energy that made her want to explode.

Bells began to move faster, and Alexis began rocking her hips furiously, pounding her body into his. Her mouth opened wider, and he pumped harder, his hand rubbing her nipples. When he rolled his tongue around her nipple, it got so hard in his mouth that Alexis could feel the spasms between her thighs.

He kissed her again, and he tasted incredible. Her body started to warm from the inside out. The feeling was overwhelming, and it caused her walls to clench hard and release spasms around his hot length. Alexis felt her walls spasming around him, and she was powerless to stop it. She could feel the desire that Bells had for her as he eased his thickness in and out of her.

"You're gonna make me come again!" she screamed. Her body began to tingle, and Alexis exploded until there was nothing but blackness.

When he rolled off her, she sat up in the bed and straddled his body and lowered herself onto him. Alexis arched her back, rotated her hips, and rode Bells as if she were an insane cowgirl in heat, and her body began to quiver again. Alexis let out the breath she'd been holding and felt overcome with the need to tell Bells that she was in love with him, but he pulled her lips to his, and he kissed her hungrily.

Slowly, Alexis began to move her hips from side to side. Bells sucked her nipples, and she moved up and down on his erection. He pushed himself as deep and as hard into her as he could. The pleasure he was giving her felt so good that when Alexis felt him swell inside of her, her walls tightened around him. She grabbed the back of his head, and he licked and sucked her nipple all while continuing to push himself inside her. Her head drifted back with her mouth open and eyes wide. Alexis was running her fingers through her hair until her entire body shook from its core. He kept pushing it to her until both screamed out. They came together in a rush, and she collapsed on his chest, but she didn't stop moving.

Satisfaction.

Chapter Four

In the morning when the first hint of sunlight crept into the suite, they made love again. Bells wanted to order room service and then spend the rest of the day making love to Alexis. She got caught up in the passion and actually considered it for a moment as he plunged deep inside her, but when it was over, Alexis fought off the urge to cuddle up against his chest and go to sleep and got out of bed.

"I have to work today."

"I understand."

"I'm going to take a shower."

"Mind if I join you?"

"Yes, I do mind if you join me." She started walking toward the bathroom. "If you join me, I just might have to take you up on your offer to make love to me all day."

"What would be so bad about that?"

"Nothing, but I have clients to see," Alexis said and shut the door.

She turned on the shower and stepped in thinking about her boss, Cynthia, because in that particular moment, she too would rather fuck than sell houses.

When Alexis got out of the shower, Bells got in, and once they were both dressed, they left the hotel. On the way to Panera to pick up her car, they listened to and chatted about the morning radio show, but there was something that Alexis felt that she had to say.

"I want you to know that I don't usually do things like this."

"Like what?"

"Like have sex with a man I just met two days ago," Alexis said and waited in vain for Bells to say, "Neither do I," before she continued. "I know that we just met, but there's . . . I don't know how to explain it, but it's like I feel a kind of energy between us."

Bells breathed a sigh of relief. "I feel it too. From the first time that I saw you sitting there at the table and you looked up and said my name, I had to ball my fists to keep my hands from shaking. I was having a rough morning in a rough week. I started to cancel, but I really wanna get a house and I needed the distraction, so I came. And then I saw you, and I was like, 'This is a diamond, a beautiful diamond.' And you're so cool, and I have enjoyed every second that we've spent together." He stopped at a red light and turned toward her. "I know this is gonna sound like some throwaway line, but I know that I found my diamond, and I never wanna spend another day without you."

Alexis melted.

Although he was right, it did sound like a throwaway line, she could feel his sincerity when he said it, and if he hadn't already won her heart, he certainly had it then. She reached over and touched his hand.

"You're right, it did sound like a line, but it may have been the sweetest thing anybody has ever said to me. I just hope that you mean it."

"I do mean it. And I'm gonna spend the rest of my life proving it to you."

"That sounded like another line," Alexis said, but again, it may have been the sweetest thing that any man had ever said to her.

When he got to Panera, Alexis got out with a promise to call him that evening when she left the office. And it was on from there between Bells and Alexis. As Bells promised, they spent each night together. When Alexis got ready to leave the office for the evening, she'd call Bells, and they'd get together and do something. It didn't matter what. They were happy doing it together. And each night, they would end up downtown, where they made love all night at the Riverfront Hyatt Regency.

"How come we never go to your place?" she asked one morning in bed.

"How come we never go to yours?"

They had been together for almost a month at that point, and neither had mentioned a word about where the other lived. "I asked you first."

"My place ain't really all that nice." He rolled closer. "Not the kind of place I would take a lady. That's why I wanna buy a house."

She gave him a quick peck on the cheek. "Stop being so picky and pick a house to buy." Alexis got out of bed and headed for the shower. When she was almost dressed and ready to go, she saw that Bells was still in bed and hadn't made a move toward the shower.

"Come on. Get up and take me to my car."

"Go ahead and take the car. The keys are on the table."

"You serious?"

"Yeah, I'm serious." He hugged the pillow and curled into the fetal position. "Take the car."

"How will you get around?"

"Hedrick will come to get me and take me home."

"Who is Hedrick?"

"That's my nigga. You'll meet him. And if I need to go somewhere, I'll drive my old BMW."

"You sure?"

"Yeah, I'm sure. Take the car."

"Okay." Alexis came to the bed and kissed him. "I'll call you later," she said and left the suite.

Although she didn't know it at the time, Alexis was driving to her car in *her* Benz A-Class. When she got home, she changed into a Misook side-tie crepe de Chine suit and went to the office. She was right about one thing—the car did say success, and Alexis was much more confident inviting clients to ride with her as she showed them properties. As time passed, her sales reflected it. As weeks turned into months, she even found a house that Bells wanted, and that forced them to have the conversation that they had both been avoiding.

"I know we haven't really talked about this, and I know that you said that you were in sales," Alexis began, and Bells chuckled.

"Yeah, about that."

"So, you wanna go ahead and tell me what I think I already know?"

"What do you think you already know?"

"That you sell drugs."

"Yes."

"So, tell me, Mr. Bell, how were you planning on buying a house? Seeing that you don't have a 'real job,'" she said, using air quotes.

"I was gonna pay cash for it like I do everything else."

Alexis dropped her head in her hands. "Let me tell you how many ways that's a bad idea."

"Why is it a bad idea?" he asked naively.

"Because transactions over ten thousand dollars have to be reported to the IRS. Do you have any credit? How did you get this car?"

"I paid cash for it."

"At a dealership?"

"No. I bought it off a friend of mine. He didn't like it, so he rarely drove it. And when he said he was gonna trade it, I offered him thirty grand in cash for it."

"Wow." Alexis dropped her head.

"Okay, so it's a bad idea." Bells paused. "You're the smart one in this relationship. You tell me how I'm gonna get that house."

"I don't know. I need to talk to some people and get some advice. I'm sure there's a way to get it done."

"I got a better idea."

"What's that?" Alexis wanted to know.

"Why don't we forget all about this house—"

Alexis quickly cut him off. "No, I'll figure something out for you," she pleaded.

"Let me finish, please." Bells paused. "We forget all about this house, and we pick something out that we both like, and you buy the house."

Alexis smiled. "I have a better idea." She paused. "Let me talk to some people and get some advice, and we'll buy our house together."

Bells smiled. "I like your idea better."

After talking to some more experienced agents about how to go about doing what she wanted to do, Alexis formed a limited liability company, Albert Bells LLC, and once she had all the proper paperwork, she opened a business account for him. Her next move was to look for cash business opportunities. The first to come along was a coin-operated laundromat. When she found out that he had some guys washing cars and selling drugs at an abandoned gas station, she got a business license and told him to stop selling drugs there, and that became his second business. The third business he bought was a vending machine business. With a legitimate source of income on paper, Alexis and Bells bought their first house, but that was just the start of it.

As Bells's legitimate and illegitimate businesses grew and expanded, he began to rely on Alexis not only for her advice and counsel, which he depended on, but her ever-improving skill at finding ways to launder the money from Bells's growing and expanding illegitimate business.

Chapter Five

They had been together for over a year when Alexis came home and found three cars that she had never seen before parked in front of her house. When she went inside, Bells and three other men she had never seen before were standing around the dining room table, and there were guns on it.

"What's going on here?" she asked tentatively as she walked into the room.

All four men looked up from what they were doing and smiled when they noticed her standing there. Bells rushed to her.

"Hey, babe, come here. There're some people I want you to meet." He took Alexis's hand and walked her to the table to introduce her to the men she would come to depend on. "This is Hedrick, Cameron, and Maxwell. Fellas, this is Diamond."

Alexis glanced at Bells and started to tell them her real name, but she wasn't fast enough.

"Finally. This is Diamond," Hedrick said, nodding his head. "This nigga been talking about you for the longest time. It's good to finally meet you."

"Yeah, Diamond, it's good to meet you," Cameron said, and Maxwell nodded and went back to loading weapons.

"Nice to meet all of you," she said, and the Diamond persona was born.

Alexis felt at a loss because, although she knew everything about his business, Bells never talked about who he was in business with.

"So, what's all this?" Alexis asked, pointing to the guns on the table.

Hedrick, Cameron, and Maxwell dropped their heads, and Bells put his arm around her. He walked her away from the table.

"Some niggas hit us today, and we gonna go back at them."

Alexis stopped and faced Bells. "You know who did it?"

"We do."

She turned toward the table. "And you know how to find them?"

"We do," he said, and Hedrick, Cameron, and Maxwell nodded in agreement because it was time for some payback.

Alexis looked at his men. "And now you're gonna ride over there and start blasting?"

"That's right."

Alexis shook her head. "Be careful."

"What?" Bells asked because he'd heard that tone of voice before.

"What?"

"What's with the head-shaking thing?"

"That's just not how I would handle it, that's all."

Bells folded his arms across his chest. "Well, how would you do it? 'Cause we gotta do something or we'll look weak."

"You ever hear the story about the two bulls?" Alexis walked to the bar and picked up a bottle of wine.

"Two bulls?" Bells questioned.

"There are two bulls standing on top of a mountain. They looked down on a valley where a dozen cows are grazing." She poured herself a glass. "The younger one says to the older one, 'Hey, let's say we run down there and fuck one of them cows.' The older one says, 'No. Let's walk down and fuck 'em all.'"

"Yeah, I heard that in some old movie I saw. What that got to do with this?"

"Let's say y'all jump in the ride and roll over there blasting. You might hit somebody, and you might not. You might hit a little girl playing in her room."

Alexis walked away from the table and sat down in the living room. She sipped her wine.

"You know who did it. You know where to find them. I think you should let the shit die down for a day or two, and then you hit them, one at a time, up close and personal."

As she talked, Bells, Hedrick, Cameron, and Maxwell slowly came toward her and listened to what she was saying. Now his men understood why Bells always heaped high praise on his Diamond and understood that she was the woman standing behind the man and what that truly meant.

"I like that, Diamond," Hedrick said.

"I do too," Bells concurred. "Let's do it."

"Good. Now y'all get them guns out of my house, please."

"Yes, ma'am," Bells said, and he, along with Hedrick, Cameron, and Maxwell, cleared the guns off the dining room table, and they left the house.

As Alexis planned, they waited and let shit die down for a couple of days before they put her plan into action. They had identified their four targets: Raymond Lucas, Alex Jackson, Danny Mason, and Logan Owens. The name of the restaurant was Uptown Kitchen and Bar on North Main Street, and that night, Raymond Lucas was sharing a meal with his girlfriend, and they were tearing up some catfish with red beans and rice. They were so into their food that neither saw Hedrick when he came in and walked straight up to the table.

"Payback time," he said before he shot Raymond Lucas in the head and rushed out of the restaurant. Cameron drove up, Hedrick got in the car, and they drove away to their next target.

Alex Jackson was a sociable, free-spirited man, kinda quiet and mystical, who could always find a reason to smile. He did business out of a club called One Up, One Down. That night was no different, as he was in his booth in a back corner of the club, sipping cocktails with three very attractive women.

"Excuse me, ladies. I need to drain the main vein," Jackson said and stood up.

"Too much information," one of the women said as he walked away from the table.

When he did, Maxwell stood up and followed him. Once Jackson was in the men's room and had stepped up to the urinal, Maxwell stepped up behind him.

"Time to die."

Maxwell shot him in the back of the head, and when his body fell to the ground, he shot him twice more before he left the men's room and walked quickly out of One Up, One Down.

Danny Mason was a soldier. You could usually find him on his corner putting in his work and making money. He was smart, energetic, and enthusiastic, and he was a very perceptive kind of guy who truly enjoyed living on the edge, so life was never boring. There was one other thing about Danny Mason: he was an arrogant fuck who didn't think he needed backup, so he worked his corner alone.

"Ain't a muthafucka stupid enough to even think about robbing me," was what he would say.

However, when Cameron and Hedrick rolled past him that day, he wasn't alone. That night, there were three other men with him.

"What you wanna do?" Hedrick asked.

"We could roll back around and blast them," Cameron suggested.

"That's exactly what Diamond wanted us to avoid, and she's right. We ride by blasting, niggas is gonna hit the deck."

"So what do you think we should do?"

"I got an idea," Hedrick said and looked at Cameron. "If you got the heart for it."

Ten minutes later, Hedrick and Cameron were walking down the street, hugged up like they were a couple. None of the men paid them any attention until it was too late. As soon as they walked up, they pulled their guns and shot Danny Mason and each of the men in the head at point-blank range.

The two men rushed back to their car and drove off.

"I got one more to do," Hedrick said as Cameron drove. "The big dog, Logan Owens."

"No, Luke Hudson is the big dog."

"Let's go end his ass anyway."

Logan Owens, the charismatic, strong-willed wannabe leader of the crew, was more of a strategic thinker with a plan for everything. Either he found a way to get it done or he made one. It had gotten late, and by that time he had heard about Raymond Lucas, Alex Jackson, and Danny Mason, so his head was on a swivel, and he saw Hedrick coming.

Owens turned around and fired at him with two guns. When Hedrick dropped to the ground, he took off running. Hedrick got up and ran after him. Owens took cover behind a car and shot back, but he missed and ran down the street. When Hedrick reached the next corner, Owens was nowhere in sight.

"Where'd he go?"

Hedrick dropped down behind a car and moved down the street slowly. Owens stood up and fired one of his guns until it was empty, and then he started running. Hedrick fired a few shots as he ran, and Owens ducked behind a car to put in his last clip. When he stood up to shoot, Hedrick put one in his head. His body dropped, and he put two more in his chest.

"He made you work for it," Cameron said when Hedrick got back in the car.

"Yeah, I had to chase his coward ass down."

It was one o'clock in the morning in the suite Alexis rented at the Riverfront DoubleTree Hotel. It was a celebration, so there was champagne and liquor and some wings she got from Publix. Hedrick, Cameron, and Maxwell were there with their girlfriends, and everybody was having a good time. Bells and Alexis were standing by the table talking when Hedrick, Cameron, and Maxwell walked up, and they raised their glasses.

"To Diamond," Hedrick said, and they drank to her.

Chapter Six

As time passed, Alexis became the brains of the operation behind the scenes, and she dealt with the contacts and the people who supplied Bells. Now, four years into their relationship, he didn't do anything without talking to her first. Things were going great. But like all great things, this too came to an end.

Bells ended the call and looked at Alexis. "Luke Hudson wants to talk."

"Not surprising. I know he's got to be reeling from the ass-kicking we dealt his people."

"Said that we can settle our differences so we can both get back to making money."

Alexis laughed. "He said that?"

"He did."

"That doesn't sound like Hudson." She shook her head. "Too enlightened. No, it's a trap, and if you go, you will be assassinated."

"I don't think so. He sounded sincere, and like you said, he's got to still be reeling from the loss we dealt him."

Although Alexis had a bad feeling about Hudson's sincerity, she didn't push the issue and began thinking about his security. "Where does he want to meet you?"

"He wants to meet at a place called Celestia's Coastal Cuisine on Dunn Avenue."

"Have you ever been there before?"

"No, have you?"

"No, I haven't been there before. We should check it out before you go."

"I'll send Maxwell to check it out," Bells said and made the call.

"You're sure about this?" she asked when he ended the call with Maxwell.

Alexis didn't think that Bells needed to meet with Hudson and thought that they should ignore the request to meet and keep doing what they were doing.

"Yeah, I'm sure."

"Okay. I still think it's a trap. Just be careful."

Bells checked his gun. "You know what a careful guy I am." He kissed her lips gently. "Everything will be fine." He kissed her again. "Trust me."

"I do trust you. It's Luke Hudson I don't trust."

Celestia's Coastal Cuisine was a cozy seafood restaurant in Jacksonville with a hip yet casual and classy environment. After Maxwell checked the place out, Bells called Hudson back, and the sit-down to settle their differences was set. When it came time to meet, Bells and Maxwell were already seated by the window when Hudson and his man showed up and got out of their car.

"Here he comes," Maxwell announced.

"I see him. Be ready for whatever," Bells said as he watched Hudson say something to the man who came with him, and then he started walking toward Celestia's by himself.

"What's up with that?" Maxwell asked when they saw him coming.

"Your guess is as good as mine. Just be ready."

As soon as Hudson stepped inside the restaurant, he raised his weapon and began shooting wildly at Bells and Maxwell. He didn't hit anything, but it did force them to drop to the floor. Bells returned his fire and hit him in the forehead. Hudson dropped the gun, and then his body fell to the ground.

"We gotta get outta here," Maxwell said as he got up from the floor.

Bells got up. "Let's go," he said, and the two men rushed to the door with their heads down and faces covered.

When they got outside, the man who came with Hudson jumped in his car and took a shot at Bells and Maxwell as he drove away. They shot back as they ran to their car, but the car made it out of the parking lot.

"How'd it go?" Alexis asked when Bells came through the door with Maxwell.

"Not good. As soon as Hudson got there, he started shooting."

"Are you all right?" she asked and rushed to him.

Bells took her in his arms and kissed her. "I'm all right, but Hudson is dead."

"I was afraid of this." She broke their embrace. "I knew something like this was going to happen."

"I know. And I should have listened to you."

They went and sat down on the couch. "I need to get ghost and lie low for a while."

"You do," Alexis agreed. "At least until we find out how much damage this is gonna cause us."

Alexis arranged for Hedrick to drive Bells to Orlando to catch a flight to the Bahamas. He was packed and ready to leave when the doorbell rang. They froze and looked at one another.

"Who could that be?" Alexis questioned and got up to see who was at the door. "It's the police."

He looked out of the window. "There are three cars out there."

"How'd they get on to you so quickly?"

"I don't know." Bells walked away from the window. "Go in the bedroom and don't come out until we're gone."

He walked to the door where she was standing. The police began banging on the door. "Police!"

Bells took her in his arms and kissed her. "I'll call the lawyer," she said as he let her go and headed toward the bedroom. Bells watched her walk to the door and turn around. Alexis waved and went into the room. When she closed the bedroom door, Bells opened the front door.

"Albert Bell?" the officer said.

"Yes."

"You're under arrest for the murder of Luke Hudson." Bells turned around, and the cops put the cuffs on him. "You have the right to remain silent. Anything you say can and will be used against you in a court of law. You have the right to speak to an attorney and to have an attorney present during any questioning."

When Alexis heard the door close, she came out of the bedroom and rushed to the window in time to see the police put Bells in the car and drive away.

"Fuck!" she shouted and went to get her phone. "Hedrick."

"What's up?"

"Bells got arrested."

"I was just about to leave to come over there. How'd the cops get on him so quick?" Hedrick asked and assumed that the man with Hudson told the police where to find Bells.

"I don't know."

"I'll be over there."

"Good. We have a lot to talk about."

When Hedrick arrived at the house with Cameron and Maxwell, they were all surprised that things happened the way they did. But not Alexis. She saw this coming and knew that Hudson would try to kill him.

"What now?" Cameron asked.

"Me and Bells had a plan in place just in case something like this happened."

"What's the plan?" Maxwell wanted to know.

"First off, I need for everybody to get new phones."

"I'll take care of that," Cameron promised.

"And the stash houses need to be moved."

"On it," Maxwell said.

"One more thing."

"What's that?" Hedrick asked.

"I need you to get all our people off the street until I say something different. Is that understood?"

"Understood."

"Y'all go handle your business," Alexis said, and the men left the house to carry out her orders.

After talking with Bells in jail, his lawyer, Elijah Oliver, called Alexis at her office, and they arranged to meet later that afternoon to discuss Bells's case. They met at Bazille, a casual and chic venue in Nordstrom in the Town Center Mall.

"To protect you and the organization, Albert plans to plead guilty to voluntary manslaughter. The prosecution offered seven years. He'll be out in five with good behavior."

"You sure that's the best you can do?"

"No, but it's what he wants. I think if we fight it and go to trial, we can beat it."

"Hudson fired first. That makes it self-defense, right?"

"I agree. But again, this is what Albert wants to do."

"Why doesn't he plead stand your ground, or something like that?"

"Stand your ground only works for white men in this country."

"So why does he want to plead guilty to voluntary manslaughter?"

"Because he thinks that's the best way to protect you and the organization. Bottom line, he doesn't want the cops to spend a lot of time digging into what y'all do and how you do it." Oliver paused. "He has a point."

"I know," Alexis said. She didn't like it, but she agreed that this was the best way to move forward. Five years wasn't all that long, and it would go by quickly. That was the way that she was looking at it.

At his arraignment and as expected, Bells pleaded guilty to voluntary manslaughter and was given a date when sentencing would take place, and he was taken back to jail. Later that same evening, in the mess hall, Bells was in line to get his food when a man walked up behind him and shoved a shank in his back. Bells pulled the shank out, turned quickly, and punched the man in the face. They fought until the guards broke it up, and Bells was taken to the infirmary, while his attacker was taken to the hole. Unfortunately, Bells had lost too much blood and died from the wound.

Alexis cried when she got the call from Detective Horace Blakey that Bells was dead. He was the love of her life, and Alexis had fallen in love with him the day they met. She missed his touch, the way he kissed her, and how he looked at her so deeply and intently that Alexis could feel the love that he had for her. She was dealing with a lot of emotions and grieving the future that they had so carefully planned for themselves.

As the weeks turned into months, her memories of Bells would come in random flashbacks that would make her giggle, or smile, or even blush at times. Other times, the onslaught of emotions out of the blue would hit her hard. During those tough days, she found comfort in Hedrick's friendship and loyalty. He and Bells went a long way back, and he would reach out to her or stop by to see if she needed anything.

"How have you been holding up? I know this hasn't been easy for you."

"I'm making it. Taking it one day at a time," Alexis said and was thankful for him.

Hedrick acknowledged what happened and gave her the space that she needed. He reassured her that what she was going through was normal and that she wasn't alone.

"Anything you need, I got you, Diamond. I promise you that."

And then they had the business to run.

"Nothing has to change," she said, and that gave Alexis purpose.

Chapter Seven

Present Day

And nothing did change. For Alexis and Hedrick, it was business as usual. Alexis called the shots, and he followed her orders. Hedrick ran things with an iron fist, and Diamond would show up when the need arose and she felt the need to personally deal with a problem. Nobody knew who she was or what her real name was, and that added to her mystique on the streets.

But now Hedrick was dead. He was tortured and murdered by Imani's boyfriend, Brock Whitehall, to ascertain their involvement in the assassination attempt on Imani's father.

She thought about sending men to kill him, but in the end, Alexis decided against it. One, she wasn't sure that her men could handle Brock, and two, she understood why he did it. He loved Imani, and when she demanded answers, her man went out and got them. Alexis remembered when a man loved her that much. Besides, Imani was like a sister to her, her best and, if she wanted to be honest, only real friend. Killing Brock would hurt Imani deeply. She would feel like such a hypocrite being the one Imani would turn to for comfort and being the one who had him killed.

She stared out the window and thought about the fact that her best friend knew so little about her. Alexis knew all about Imani's life, and that included her illegal businesses. Imani was a gunrunner, and her brother Hareem was a drug dealer. Even though Alexis didn't see it that way, he was her competition. Because of that, Hareem had been waging a cold war of sorts, doing things to provoke Alexis into meeting with him. That wasn't something that she had any interest in doing. She couldn't imagine how betrayed Imani would feel when she found out the truth.

You should be the one to tell her.

Alexis glanced over at Cameron as he drove. Although he was anxious to step up and fill the void that Hedrick's death left, she knew that he couldn't do what Hedrick did for her. He was a good man, though. He was loyal, and she trusted him.

She looked at her watch. It was getting late, and Alexis wanted to get some sleep that night, at least more sleep than she got the night before. But this was important, and important things needed to be dealt with.

Marques Hampton and Von Slaughter had staged a robbery. The two had arranged it so that Angela would find them tied up on the floor with the front door kicked in and the dope and the money gone. They might have gotten away with it if Marques hadn't told Angela the truth, and she knew enough to call Alexis right away.

One of the worst feelings in the world was thinking that you got away with something and then finding out that you didn't. That was about to happen to Von Slaughter.

He was with his on-again, off-again woman, Carleitha. They had invited to her house a few close friends who shared their passion for sex and drugs, and they were celebrating the deception. They were on-again, off-again because Carleitha was a crackhead who would smoke up all his dope, and the cycle began. He would get tired of her shit and swear that he was done with her. But once he made up his loss and got back in Diamond's good graces, like the snake she was, Carleitha would come slithering back. Only this time, she got him hooked, too.

That was the reason that he had to talk Marques into the fake robbery. Slaughter and Carleitha had one of their parties that lasted three days, and they wiped out a chunk of product. Knowing that he couldn't make up that loss before Diamond found out and killed him, staging the robbery seemed like the best and only way out.

But as far as Slaughter was concerned, that was all behind him now, and since he had set aside some product for personal consumption from the fake robbery, it was time to get loose and have a good time.

In attendance that night were the usual suspects: Art and Elaine and Shawnta and Vienna. They were all naked, sitting around the coffee table, smoking the pile of rocks their hosts had cooked up for them. After a while, they moved the coffee table because it was in the way.

Slaughter and Carleitha were sitting on the couch, and Art and Elaine were on their knees. Elaine was between Carleitha's thighs, tonguing her clit, and Art was sucking Slaughter's dick. Shawnta and Vienna were on their knees too. They had strapped up. Shawnta was fucking Elaine, and Vienna was fucking Art when Alexis walked in with Cameron.

"What the fuck kinda freaky shit we got going on here?" she asked Cameron and took out her gun. Alexis fired two shots at the ceiling.

Everybody stopped what they were doing.

"Diamond," Slaughter said and tried to cover himself with his hands.

She looked at the six of them, and then her eyes zeroed in on the little bit of rock that was left on the table. Alexis shook her head. "I don't know who y'all are, but you need to leave. Now."

Art, Elaine, Shawnta, and Vienna didn't have to be asked twice. While Cameron pointed two guns at them, they got dressed as quickly as they could. Since Alexis had no idea what went on and where before she got there, she wasn't about to sit down anywhere in the living room. Alexis got a chair from the dining room and dragged it into the living room. She placed the chair in front of the couch, wiped it off, and sat down. She pointed her gun at Slaughter and Carleitha.

"What's this about?" Slaughter asked because he was sure that he had gotten away with the fake robbery. He and Carleitha had both gotten pillows to cover themselves with.

"Ask me a stupid question like that again and I will shoot your dick off."

Once Cameron had seen Art, Elaine, Shawnta, and Vienna to the door, he issued a warning. "She may not know who the fuck y'all are, but I do, and I know where to find and kill you." They left, and he returned to the living room and pointed both of his guns at Slaughter and Carleitha.

"You wanna tell me why I'm here, Carleitha?" Alexis asked calmly.

She said nothing. Now that Elaine was no longer between Carleitha's thighs, she was eyeing the last of the rock on the table and hoping that she lived through whatever Alexis had planned for Slaughter.

"Marques already told me everything, so you might as well admit what you did to me, and we can talk about how you're gonna make restitution."

"It was her fault, Diamond," Slaughter said quickly and pointed at her.

"My fault?" Carleitha shouted. "Nigga, you was sitting there smoking right along with me. Don't put that shit on me."

"Shut the fuck up, Carleitha!" Alexis said. "You had your chance to talk, and you didn't have shit to say."

"We got a little carried away, and that was the only way, but I swear, Diamond, it won't happen again." Slaughter looked at Carleitha. "I need to be done with you for real this time and get back to doing what's important."

"Still trying to put that shit on me. I ain't have nothing to do with faking no robbery, but the shit is my fault."

"Shut up!" Slaughter shouted. He put his hands up. "Give me a chance, Diamond. I can come back from this. You know I can."

"Maybe you could have years ago, but now?" She shook her head. "I don't think so. You used to be a good man, someone I thought was solid, but that man hasn't existed in a long time, has he, Cameron? You ain't no better than her now."

She looked over at Carleitha. "And I gave you every chance to get yourself right. So, you've had your chance, and you let this loser take you down."

Alexis shot Carleitha in the head.

Her blood splattered on his face.

Slaughter put his hands together and begged. "Please, Diamond, give me one more chance."

Alexis shot Slaughter in the head.

"Get rid of it and the bodies and burn the couch," she said to Cameron, handing him the gun and walking toward the door.

Chapter Eight

After another long day at the real estate office, Alexis pulled her Avalon Hybrid into the garage and turned off the car. As soon as she stepped inside and closed the door, Alexis kicked out of her Dolce & Gabbana stiletto pumps and plopped down in her favorite chair. For the next fifteen minutes, she sat there quietly thinking before she got up and headed for the bathroom, taking off her Vince belted satin blazer and skirt on the way.

Alexis turned on the water to take the long, hot bath that she had been thinking about all day. While the water ran, Alexis dropped a Nubian Heritage African black soap bubble bath bomb into the tub. She went to the bar and poured herself a glass of 2019 Livio Felluga pinot grigio and returned to the bathroom to soak, sip wine, and put the day behind her. Since she was out late the last three nights and she didn't get a lot of sleep, her plan for the evening was simple: a hot bath and then bed.

Alexis had been in the tub long enough for the water to start to get cold when her cell phone rang. She could tell by the ring tone that the call was from Cameron, and he was calling for Diamond. Since Bells died, she'd always had two phones, one for Alexis and a separate one just for Diamond, and not many people had that number. Alexis gave serious consideration to not answering it, especially since the phone was in the bedroom, and she was thinking about adding some hot water so she could stay in the tub longer.

As the phone continued to ring and eventually went to voicemail, Alexis got out of the bathtub and dried herself off. She moisturized her skin before she returned Cameron's call.

"Hello."

"What's up?"

"I need to see you."

"Where are you?"

"At the crib."

"Give me an hour."

"I'll be here," Cameron promised, and Alexis ended the call.

"Shit," she cursed quietly because she was tired and didn't want to go out that night. "This better be important," she said and went to make up her face and get dressed.

She selected a red Yves Saint Laurent halter O-ring jumpsuit and Christian Louboutin Rosalie iridescent leather slingback sandals, put on enough diamonds and jewelry to live up to her name, put on a pair of oversized round acetate light-adaptive sunglasses, and was out the door. Alexis got in her Jaguar F-Type coupe and drove to Cameron's apartment to see what he wanted.

When she arrived at Cameron's apartment, Alexis was surprised to see that Tyrone Winder, Hedrick's lieutenant, was there with Byron Ross.

"What's up, Diamond?" Winder said, and she nodded her head.

"I need to speak with you, Cameron," she said and went into the bedroom. She stood holding the door until Cameron joined her, and then she closed the door. "Why are they here?"

"He's here because he needs to step into Hedrick's position and run his crew."

Alexis shook her head. "No, Cameron, I need you to step into Hedrick's position. Sure, Winder can step up and run Hedrick's crew. I expected no less. But what is not gonna happen is him thinking that he is gonna slide into Hedrick's lieutenant's spot."

"I understand."

"Do you? Do you really understand that now that Hedrick is dead, I need to depend on you and Maxi more than I ever have?"

"I know. That's why I thought the bringing in Winder and Ross might be a good thing."

"No. Bringing in Winder and Ross is not a good thing because I don't need them. You know me well enough to know that you don't need to bring people around who I don't normally do business with. Despite the fact that he's been working for us for years, I don't know that man, and I don't know if I can trust him. And I need to be able to trust the people who are closest to me. That's you, Cameron, and Maxi. That's it. Maybe at some point in the future, Winder might prove that he is somebody I could trust." Alexis shook her head. "But not now."

"I understand."

"Good. Go get Maxi."

Alexis sat down on the bed and waited for Cameron to return with Maxwell.

"You wanted to see me, Diamond?" Maxwell stuck his head in the door.

"Yes, both of you come in and shut the door."

Maxwell looked over his shoulder at Winder, grinned, and closed the door. "What's up?" he asked.

"Like I was telling Cameron, now that Hedrick is dead, I need to depend on you and him more than I ever have."

"I'm ready."

"I know you are, Maxi. And that is why I need you to deal with Winder, Ross, and the rest of Hedrick's people. You ready for that?"

"Hell, yeah, I'm ready for that." Like Cameron was anxious to prove himself after living for years in Hedrick's shadow, Maxwell was anxious to emerge from that shadow as well. He was happy with the confidence that Alexis was showing in him. "I won't let you down."

"I know that you won't." Alexis turned toward Cameron. "What else do you need?"

"That was it," Cameron said.

"Okay." Alexis stood up. "What I need from you both is to make decisions, not call me and ask what you should do. Make a decision and let me know what you decide to do. If I don't approve of what you did, I will let you know, but I trust you. Just like I trusted Hedrick to make decisions, I trust the two of you. Are we clear about that?"

"Yeah, Diamond, we're clear," Maxwell said, excited about his opportunity to show and prove.

"What about you, Cam? You ready to move this thing forward?"

"You know I am."

"Good. I'm out." Alexis pointed in Cameron's face. "Deal with them niggas."

"I will," Cameron said to her as Alexis left the bedroom and headed toward the door without so much as a glance in Winder and Ross's direction.

"What the . . ." Winder said when the apartment door closed and Cameron and Maxwell came out of the bedroom. "Where is she going?"

"I didn't ask, and she didn't say," Cameron said.

"I needed to talk to her," Winder protested angrily. He felt totally disrespected that she wouldn't even look in his direction, much less speak to him.

Maxwell laughed. "No, you didn't. You just thought you wanted to talk to Diamond, but actually it was me you needed to talk to all along."

"Fuck you talking about, nigga?"

"You need anything, you come to me. That's what I'm talking about, nigga."

"So, I work for you now? Is that what this is about?" Winder asked.

"No," Cameron said quickly because all Maxwell was doing was throwing gas on the burning blaze that was Winder. "You work for Diamond, just like you did when you walked in here."

"Then why won't the bitch show me enough respect to talk to me? Acknowledge my presence and that I make her bitch ass a bunch of money?" Winder said, and Maxwell took out his gun and pressed the barrel to Winder's head. Ross put his hand on his gun.

"Call Diamond a bitch again, muthafucka, and see how much longer you live."

Winder put up his hands. "Take it easy."

Cameron stepped toward him and moved Maxwell's gun away from Winder's head. "We not gonna have that disrespect."

"Disrespect? Disrespect is treating a nigga like he ain't even here. As much muthafuckin' money I make for her, least she could do is speak to a nigga."

"She could, you right, she could, but that ain't Diamond. She is funny that way. She doesn't fuck with people she doesn't know."

"That's the thing. I been knowing her for years, as much muthafuckin' money I make for her ass."

"No, you been knowing Hedrick for years," Cameron said. He was tired of going around in this circle. "Look, I hear you, but bottom line, Diamond doesn't know you, and she ain't gonna fuck with you on that level until that changes, period. End of fuckin' story." Cameron looked at Ross. "If you can't deal with that simple fact, maybe some changes need to be made."

"Naw," Winder said and started toward the door. "We good."

"Good," Cameron said.

"I'll get with you two tomorrow," Maxwell said with his gun still in his hand and followed them out of the apartment.

Chapter Nine

"As long as you show Diamond respect, I promise everything is gonna be all right between us," Maxwell said to Winder and Ross as they walked toward their car.

"I didn't mean her no disrespect, but be honest, the way Diamond played me was fuckin' disrespectful."

"True that, true that. It was, but that is just how she is, how she's always been since Bells got killed." Maxwell stepped up to Winder. He still had the gun in his hand. "But you and I ain't gonna have no problem, right?"

"Like I said, it's all good." Winder unlocked the car door, and Ross got in. "As long as you show me respect, we ain't gonna have no problems."

"Long as you respect me, and you never disrespect Diamond again, we ain't gonna have no problems. Cool?"

"Like I said, it's all good."

"Then I'll get with you two tomorrow," Maxwell said and finally put his gun away. Winder got in the car, started it up, and drove off.

"Fuck that bitch! That's right, I said it. Fuck that bitch! Fuck that bitch and the high and mighty horse she rode in on, you hear me! Who the fuck does she think she is?" Winder asked. "I should have put a bullet in her brain."

"But you didn't. You stood there and took it like—"

"Like a what?"

"Like a man who knows where his paper comes from."

"Okay. Was I wrong?"

"No, you wasn't wrong. I'm just saying that you stood there and took it, that's all. No point crying about it, especially since you didn't put a bullet in her brain and you're not going to."

He raised his gun as he drove. "I may not put a bullet in her brain for disrespecting me, but you, nigga . . ." Winder joked.

"Whatever, muthafucka. And be careful how you swing that gat around. Accidents do happen."

Winder put the gun down. "What you getting ready to do?"

"Nothing. Take me home."

"You got it. But tomorrow when Maxwell starts talking that shit, he will catch a bullet," he said and dropped Ross off at his girlfriend Gail Smith's apartment.

Ross and Gail were both deep in the game, but they were both tired of it. They had saved some cash and were thinking about getting out and going legit. They had been talking about it for months, and in light of the way things were going—Hedrick dead, Diamond acting funny, and Winder's volatile temper—maybe it was time to get serious about it.

"Hey, babe," Gail said when he came through the door and tossed his keys in the dish.

"Hey."

"How'd it go with Diamond?"

"It didn't."

"What you mean it didn't?"

"I mean she wouldn't even talk to us." He kissed her and went into the kitchen.

"What you mean she wouldn't talk to y'all?"

He got a bottle of beer from the refrigerator and closed the door. "We at Cam's crib, Diamond walks in, takes a look at me and Winder sitting there, she looks at Cam and says, 'I need to speak with you, Cameron,' and she took her ass in the bedroom."

"And?"

"And nothing. When she came out, she left without a word."

Gail shook her head. "That's just fuckin' disrespectful. I know Winder was hot."

"He was talking about killing Diamond over it."

"So, what's up? How'd y'all leave it?"

"Even though they didn't say it, we work for Maxwell now."

"I know that had to piss Winder off, too."

"He didn't say anything about that. Too busy talking shit about how Diamond dissed him."

"Even if he didn't say anything about it, you know that nigga is crazy." Gail got up from the couch and went to get another beer. "He will do some shit that will affect all of us."

"You don't think I know that?" Ross said louder than he needed to.

"I'm just sayin'."

"I know, and I'm sorry." He drained the bottle. "This shit got me thinking." Gail returned and handed him the bottle. "Thank you."

"You're welcome." Gail sat down next to him. "What you been thinking?"

"I've been thinking that shit's been good between us lately."

"We have been on a good run, haven't we?" Gail acknowledged because it wasn't always like that.

Ross and Gail had been together for almost fourteen years at that point. They loved each other, that was never a question, but in the early years of their relationship, each had a wandering eye and was more than willing to explore their passions with other partners. Of course, it caused problems in the relationship for them, but their love for one another and the intensity of the love Ross and Gail had when they made up was always enough to keep them together.

But something happened when they had a fight over her infidelity on his thirtieth birthday. Ross told her that she needed to grow up and get serious about life. Gail's response was to tell him that he needed to grow up and get serious about life too. Although both knew that the other was right, that they both needed to grow up and get serious about life, the fight raged out of control for another hour or so, and then they had makeup sex, it was great, and they drifted off to sleep. When they woke up, it was as if they had awakened to a new reality between them, and they began to focus on each other. Interestingly enough, the improvement in their relationship proved to be good for business.

"But with shit going the way it's going, I was thinking that maybe it's time for us to think about doing something else."

"Like what?"

"I'm talking about getting out and doing something else."

"You serious?"

"Yeah, babe, I'm serious. We got some cash saved and money in the bank."

A few years ago, Gail started working at a fast-food restaurant where she sold rocks and powder out of the drive-through, and her check was direct deposited. When she stopped working there, she kept making small deposits in that account, and now they had just over $16,000 in the bank.

"We could get out, go somewhere, and start over."

"We could go back to North Carolina, to Williamston," Gail suggested. It was her hometown, and she still had family and plenty of friends there.

"We could do that." Ross had been home with her many times, and her family loved him. If that was where Gail wanted to go, he could see himself living there. "We could definitely do that."

"But what would we do?"

"We could do whatever we wanted to. I'm pretty good with cars. I could open a garage. And you could open the day care center that you always used to talk about."

Gail laughed. "I haven't thought about that in years. I'm surprised that you remembered." She thought about it. "But I do love kids, so it is definitely something to think about."

Ross moved closer and kissed her on the cheek. "Maybe we could even think about having some of our own."

"I like that idea."

"So, we gonna do it?"

"Yes." She kissed him. "Yes. Let's do it."

"Great!" He kissed her.

"You gonna tell Winder?" she asked, and their lips met again.

"Hell no." Ross ran his fingers through Gail's hair and pulled her closer. "We gonna hit this thing hard for the next couple of months, and then we outta here like two thieves in the night."

"We do our best shit at night," she said and began unbuttoning his shirt, and it wasn't very long after that that they were naked.

Ross licked two fingers and began to gently massage Gail's clit while running his tongue along her lips, and then made tight circles around her clit. When he eased one finger inside her, she was so wet that it made him want to rise up and plunge his dick deep inside her, but that would ruin the moment, and he wanted to make it last.

Her mouth and eyes opened wide, and she grabbed his head as her head drifted back, and she came hard from the pleasure he had given her. She pushed him away and sprang to her feet, took him by the hand, and led him to the bed.

When Ross crawled onto the bed next to her, their lips met again, and they got lost in the sensation of her lips against his. She kissed and tongued her way down to his erection. He closed his eyes and felt her. Felt her lips, soft and wet, slowly sliding up and down on his erection. She sucked slowly up and down, and then in circles around his head.

Gail clasped her fingers together and placed them around his throbbing erection and slowly moved her hands up and down. With her thumb and forefinger, she squeezed the bottom of his shaft, causing the head to swell. She ran circles around the head with her tongue, and then she slid her moistened lips down on him. Up and down, deeper and deeper, slowly, until she had taken almost all of him in her mouth. She looked deeply into his eyes, and he got overwhelmed, watching as she ran her tongue over her lips and gently kissed his head. Then he thought that he heard a noise in the apartment.

"Shhh," Ross said softly and listened carefully.

Gail raised her head. "What?"

He heard the sound again. "Someone is in here," Ross said and got out of bed.

"You sure?"

Ross put his pants on, got his gun, and as Gail got up and began getting dressed, he left the room. He saw that there were three of them. One of the men came into the living room and shot at him. Ross returned fire and ran for cover as Gail came out of the bedroom with her nine. She looked for Ross. He was running down the hallway.

"There's three of them! Don't let them get away!" he yelled.

Gail could see that the balcony door was open. *That's how they got in,* she thought and heard shots being fired. She ran in that direction and saw someone run into the dining room. Gail fired and hit him with two shots to his chest. Gail shot him again, kicked his gun away, and kept moving toward the hallway.

"Ross!" she yelled, but he didn't answer.

Gail heard footsteps coming up behind her. When she turned, she saw one man shoot Ross, and he went down. The men turned and fired at Gail. She ducked back into the hallway and shot back blindly. She looked at Ross's body on the floor. She was running out of bullets and knew that she had to get out of there. Gail made a run for the door but got hit with three shots in the back before she got there.

The two remaining shooters stood over Ross and Gail's bodies and shot them twice more in the chest.

"Let's get Griff's body and get outta here."

"Help me carry him. The nigga is heavier than he looks."

Chapter Ten

It was early in the day the first time Cameron called. Alexis sent the call to voicemail and continued showing the Stevenses the property so they could make an eleven o'clock flight back to Wisconsin. It was ten minutes later when Cameron called again, and once again, Alexis glanced at the display and sent him to voicemail. She had just told the Stevenses about the marble countertops throughout the house when her phone rang again.

"I understand if you need to take that," Mr. Stevens said, and his lovely wife nodded in agreement.

"I'm sorry. I'll only be a minute," Alexis said and took the call as she walked away. "What's up?" she asked softly.

"Ross is dead."

"That's the guy who was with Winder last night, right?"

"Yeah."

"I'll call you back."

Alexis ended the call and quickly made another. It went to voicemail. "It's Alexis. Call me back please." She ended the call and returned to the Stevenses. "I am so sorry about that."

"It's quite all right," Mrs. Stevens said. "It gave us a chance to talk among ourselves, and we think that we'd like to make an offer."

"Excellent," Alexis said and went into negotiating mode.

Once she had taken the Stevenses back to the office, they rescheduled their flight back to Wisconsin, and she got things moving on their offer, Alexis tried her call again.

This time, he answered. "I thought I'd be hearing from you today."

Alexis stood up and left the Stevenses in her office so she could talk. "Did you get my message?" she asked.

"No. I haven't checked my voicemail today."

"I need to see you."

"The usual spot in an hour."

"Make it two."

"That's even better."

"See you then," Alexis said and ended the call.

Once she got her things together, Alexis turned off her computer and left for the night. It was forty-five minutes later that she was parking in the garage in downtown Jacksonville. When she came out of the garage, she walked down South Newnan Street to the Northbank Riverwalk. She leaned against the rail in front of the Hyatt Regency and looked out at the St. Johns River. Alexis had been standing there for a while when a man walked up and leaned against the rail nearby.

"How are you, Alexis?" asked Detective Horace Blakey.

"I've been better, Horace."

When Bells was murdered in jail, it was the detective who came to the house to notify Alexis. It was also the day that he notified her that he was Bells's police contact and had been for years. Over the years, they had gotten very close.

"How's it going with you?" Alexis asked the detective, who had gotten to be something of a father figure to her.

"Counting the days until I turn in my shield and call it a career."

"What are you gonna do?"

"Garden."

"Gardening, you?"

"Yeah, me, gardening."

"You just don't seem like the green thumb type is all."

"Well, I am. But enough of that shit. You wanna know about Byron Ross and Gail Hopkins."

"Yes, but I do care about what you have planned for the future."

"Right. I love you too."

Alexis smiled. "Tell me what I came to hear, old man."

"No signs of forced entry. It appears that the killer came in through the balcony. Looks like they capped one of the shooters, because there was a large blood stain on the carpet but no body. Police confiscated two kilos, a little less than ten thousand dollars in cash, and a stash of weapons."

"So, it wasn't a robbery."

"No, it wasn't. Looks like you have an enemy who isn't interested in taking your money."

"They get anywhere finding out who murdered Kevin Hedrick?" she asked even though she already knew.

"The investigation hit a dead end. No witnesses, no clues. Whoever did it was thorough."

"Thanks, Horace," Alexis said, reaching into the Jacquemus Le Bisou Mousqueton shoulder bag that she was carrying and taking out an envelope. She dropped it on the ground and walked away. When she did, Blakey picked up the envelope, and he walked in the opposite direction. Now that she knew what she needed to know, Alexis called Cameron back as soon as she got in her car.

"What's up?"

"Meet me at the condo in an hour," she said and ended the call.

After Bells was murdered and Alexis made the decision to stay in the game, she had decided that she needed to separate her two lives as much as possible. That meant that Diamond needed a place of her own. So, she created shell companies to buy a two-bedroom, two-bath space on the thirty-first floor with a large wraparound balcony with a southwest view of the city and its own private elevator in the Peninsula Condominiums on the south bank in San Marco. When she got there, Alexis changed into a cream stone Barefoot Dreams pashmina cape and drawstring sweatshirt and waited for Cameron to arrive.

While she waited, Alexis thought about Hedrick and the day that he let her know that he knew about her other life. Bells had been dead for a couple of years at that point when Hedrick began to get curious about why it was so hard to reach Alexis during the day. And when he finally did reach her, her line was always the same.

"I'll call you back."

So, he followed her over the course of a week and was able to find out that by day she was Alexis Fox, a successful real estate agent. Therefore, the next time he called and she said that she would call him back, Alexis was surprised by what he had said.

"Make it fast, Alexis. This is important."

"Excuse me, what did you say?"

"Alexis. That's your name, ain't it?"

"Yes, but—"

"Your secret's safe with me. Now, go on and finish up with your client and call me back," was what Hedrick had told her that day.

The doorbell rang, and she got up, wondering if it was time to tell Cameron who she really was.

"What's up, Diamond?" Cameron said when she opened the door.

"Come in." Alexis stepped aside and allowed him to come in. "Have a seat."

"Thanks," he said, and they sat down in the living room.

"You know what happened?"

"Winder said that when he rolled by there this morning to pick Ross up, the cops were there."

"You know who did it?"

"Nope, but I think it's Hareem, Martel, and them who did it. Gotta be."

"I don't think so."

"Why not?"

"Because the police confiscated two kilos and damn near ten thousand dollars in cash of my money. If it was Hareem and them, why leave the product and the cash for the cops to find?"

"True."

"No. This is somebody else. I need you to find out who."

"It may be over some shit that Ross and Gail were into," Cameron suggested. "Gail used to be out there. You know what I'm sayin'? Used to drive that nigga crazy."

"If I remember correctly, Ross wasn't sitting home waiting for her. He was out there cheating on Gail just like she was cheating on him."

"True."

"Find out if it was some of their personal shit that got them killed or if it was business."

"If it was business, why leave the dope and the money?" Cameron stood up. "I think you're right. This was some of Ross's and Gail's personal shit."

Alexis stood up and pointed in Cameron's face. "Be sure."

"I got you, Diamond." He started for the door. "But just to be sure, I'm gonna ask around about Hareem and them. Just in case there was another reason to kill Ross and Gail and not take the money and the product."

"I was thinking the same thing."

Alexis walked Cameron to the door, thinking that he might be all right filling Hedrick's shoes after all, and she might be able to trust him with her secret one day in the future. She closed the door and went to change back into her business suit to meet Imani.

Chapter Eleven

Martel Gresham turned off of Palm Forest Place onto the long driveway and drove past the circle with a water fountain that was surrounded by palm trees. He parked in front of the Mosley's fabulous seven-bedroom home that Alexis sold them in Ponte Vedra Beach, a beachfront community southeast of the city.

"Morning, Miss Kimberly," he said politely when she opened the door.

"Morning, Martel," their housekeeper, Kimberly, said and stepped aside.

Martel stepped into the foyer and looked up at the Crystal Rain chandelier that hung over the spiral design on the granite floor and the spiral staircase with marble rails that wrapped around the wall.

I could get used to living like this, he thought as Kimberly closed the door.

"Hareem is in the great room with Omeika."

"Thank you." Martel started for the great room, and Kimberly walked alongside him. "How are you this morning?" he asked respectfully.

"I'm fine. Thank you for asking," she replied as they separated, and she returned to the kitchen.

"What's up, Hareem?"

"Marty-mar! What's up?"

"Ain't nothing," he said and went to Omeika's playpen and leaned in. "How are you, adorable?"

Omeika made noises and touched his face. "Tell Uncle Marty-mar you're fine," her father said, shocked because Omeika usually cried anytime Martel came near her. Martel sat down on the couch next to Hareem.

Martel was Hareem Mosley's right- and left-hand man. They had known each other since they were kids. They started out in the game together, selling what little bit of dope that Hareem could steal from his father until they had made enough money to buy weight for themselves.

When Mr. O got run out of Miami and moved to Jacksonville, Hareem saw it as his opportunity to step into the void when they decided to get out of the retail end of the game and go back to their core business: sale and distribution. He called his boys up from Miami and broke into the Jacksonville market. The Miami boys came in hot and hard with a high-quality product, and with the firepower supplied by Imani to back him up, they went major.

"What's up with you?"

Hareem spread his arms. "Me and my girl chillin'. That's what's up."

"I hear you."

"Everything going good with you?" Hareem asked.

When Hedrick was eliminated, everybody expected Hareem to take down Cameron and move a step closer to either bringing Diamond on board or pushing her out of the market. But that didn't happen. He was a father now, and since he had grown up without a father for most of his life, that meant something to Hareem. His focus became ensuring that Omeika wouldn't grow up aspiring to run a criminal organization as he and Imani had. Therefore, Hareem chose to spend the majority of his time being Omeika's father, so he stepped back and handed power to Martel.

"Everything is lovely. Since you killed Hedrick, things have been splendid," Martel said.

When Brock killed Hedrick, everybody assumed that it was Hareem who had done it because he believed that he was the target of the assassination attempt and his father was hit instead. He went along with it, and Brock, being the person he was, never told anybody different.

"The nigga had to go," Hareem boasted.

"Tell the truth. Did you go after Hedrick 'cause he shot your daddy, or because he thought Omeika was his baby?"

"Both."

Martel laughed. "Bullshit, nigga! I know you. You killed that nigga 'cause he was fuckin' Loonie."

Lucinda Thompson, who everybody called Loonie, used to be with Hareem, but when she got pregnant with his baby, Loonie left Jacksonville and ran home to her mom's house in Palatka, a city sixty-two miles south of Jacksonville. That was where she met Hedrick, and he believed that the baby was his until the day she was born.

"I knew that wasn't none of my baby the second I saw her. I didn't know it was that nigga's baby. I just knew it wasn't none of mine," was what Hedrick had told Brock before Brock killed him.

"Naw. The shit was strictly business," Hareem said, hoping that Martel would let it go.

"Whatever, nigga. I'ma let you have that. But you and I know what's real."

"Good. So, what's up?"

"I wanna know what you wanna do about Diamond."

"What about Diamond?"

"I hear that since you killed Hedrick, some of her people are dissatisfied."

"Who are we talking about?"

"Winder, Henderson, a couple of others. Word is that, without Hedrick, Diamond's getting weak. She's counting on pretty boy Cameron to step up, and he always was a pussy, so the nigga can't handle it."

"That makes sense," Hareem said, feeling thankful to Brock for killing Hedrick. Omeika started to cry. He got up, picked up her bottle, and got her from the playpen. "He ran shit for her."

"I think we should step it up. Now's the time to wipe them niggas out and be done with it."

"No." Hareem gave Omeika the bottle. "Don't kill them. Recruit them. That's how you take over her business without firing a shot."

"Much easier to just kill them all."

"I know, Marty-mar, I know." Hareem laughed and sat down with Omeika. "I know your murderous ass would rather murder them all, but going to war is bad for business."

"I know that ain't you talking that 'bad for business' shit. That's Imani talking."

"Yeah, but when she's right, she's right, and my pops agrees."

"That shit's funny, way your pops used to run Miami."

"Everybody gets older and wiser. You and me need to do shit smarter if we gonna get old and respectable in the game."

"Like your pops," Martel said because he had a lot of respect and admiration for the violent way Mr. O used to run his program in Miami before he got old and got run out by younger, more violent men. "All right, baby boy. We do shit Imani's way and back off Diamond." He chuckled. "Live and let live."

"Like I said, focus on recruiting them."

"That's how you take over her business without firing a shot." Martel stood up. "I'm out," he said as Hareem's phone rang.

He repositioned Omeika and answered the phone. "What's up, Jamarcus?"

"You heard Hedrick's boy, Ross, and his woman got killed last night?"

"No, this the first I'm hearing about it," he said and looked at Martel. "Marty-mar's here, and he ain't say nothing about that."

"What?"

"Somebody killed Ross and his woman last night."

Martel held up his right hand. "Wasn't me."

"Diamond know who did it?"

"I ain't heard anything about that, but you know she gonna think we did it."

"Did you?" Hareem asked Martel.

"Hell no. You said back off Diamond for a minute."

"Thanks, Jamarcus. Let me know if you hear anything else."

"Will do," Jamarcus said, and Hareem ended the call.

Hareem sat quietly, thinking about what he'd just heard and what it meant to him.

"What you thinking?" Martel asked.

"That she can't keep her people safe." Hareem nodded confidently. "That makes this the time to go hard at recruiting Diamond's people."

"On it. I'll holla at you later," Martel said and left the room, passing Brock on his way out of the house. "What's up, Brock?"

"Marty-mar, what's up?" he said and walked to the door with Martel.

The two men shook hands before Martel left. Brock closed the door. He'd overheard the conversation about Diamond and had some unanswered questions of his own. He had been wondering how Diamond knew Mr. O had been shot, unless she heard it from somebody who was there at the party. He thought back to the night that he tortured and killed Hedrick. He had just wheeled out a cart with a battery and some cables on it.

"Did you try to kill Hareem and hit his father instead?" Brock asked that night.

"Look, man. It wasn't me. I didn't even know it was the nigga's birthday or where his daddy lives. And even if I did wanna kill him, Diamond told us to back off."

That made Brock pause. "When did she do that?"

"Same day it happened."

Brock picked up the cables. "What did she say?"

"She asked me if it was me. I didn't know what the fuck she was talking about. She told me his daddy got shot and for me not to do anything. But fuck that! I wasn't gonna be no pussy about it. He hit us. We busted back."

Having found out what he wanted to know, Brock put a bullet in his forehead and returned Hedrick's body to where he picked him up, displaying his body for his crew to find. Brock had reviewed the names on the guest list and had spoken to some of them, but so far, none of the guests stood out. It never occurred to him that Alexis, who twisted her ankle when the shooting broke out and she tried to run, was the one he was looking for.

Chapter Twelve

"Imani!" Brock shouted as he walked through the house.

"I'm in the office," Imani shouted back.

"She's in the office," Hareem said as Brock passed the great room.

"What's up, Hareem?"

"How you livin', Brock?"

"Like the princes we are," Brock said and kept heading toward the office.

Imani had been in love with Brock Whitehall since she was 15 years old and he started working for her father. Those days, Brock barely noticed her, and when he did, he treated her like the little girl she was. When he went to prison for her father, she was 17, but when Brock got out ten years later and saw Imani, she could tell by the way that he was staring at her that he no longer saw her as a little girl.

His look screamed, "I want you," which was good because she wanted him too. And now that they were together, she couldn't get enough of him.

Imani was in the office that she shared with her father. When Brock came into the room, Imani got up and came from behind the desk. She all but rushed into his arms, threw her arms around his neck, and kissed him passionately, remembering the love they made the night before.

Last night at his place, Brock attacked her tongue the way she liked it before he lifted her legs and thrust himself into her. She kissed and sucked his neck and rocked her hips while he pushed himself deeper inside her. It sent a sensation rushing through her body, and the feeling was indescribable. When he felt her juices drenching his shaft again, he began to pound his stiff dick into her dripping wet pussy, all the while enjoying the view of her perfect body.

Imani made slow circles around his nipples, and they got harder for her. She spread her legs wider, and he continued to ease himself in and out of her, and then after a few long strokes, he pulled out of her and began fingering her clit. She was amazed at how hungry, damn near desperate she felt to have him inside her once again. Brock played with her lips and used his fingers to hold her lips apart. He slid his tongue inside her and tasted her sweetness again. He licked Imani's clit with the tip of his tongue until it began to swell, and he felt her body quiver.

Just thinking about it made Imani's body tremble with anticipation of them doing it again. She thought about grabbing Brock by the hand and dragging him upstairs to the bedroom that she rarely used these days so he could take her.

"Good morning," she cooed.

"You said that earlier."

Brock wanted Imani too. The more he thought about her body pounding against him, the more he wanted to push her over the desk and plunge deep inside her.

Imani started to say something, but it was as if the words got caught in her throat.

"What?" he asked.

"Nothing," she said, quickly broke their embrace, and went to sit down. "Did you get that taken care of?"

Brock sat down in front of the desk. "Done." He'd gotten up early that morning to drive to Daytona Beach to meet a client about a shipment of an Israeli-made weapon, the IWI Galil Ace pistol. "Wright said to tell you hello. He'll take delivery next Wednesday."

"Perfect." Imani turned to her computer and clicked the mouse a few times. "All we need is for Robinson to take the shipment of HK433s we talked about when we met him in Atlanta and this will be a great month." Imani spun around and smiled playfully at Brock. "It's the kind of month that makes the boss think about taking her boy toy to the islands for the weekend."

"Boy toy?" Brock laughed. "As long as you're talking about this boy toy—"

"I only have one."

"Then I'm all for it."

"What you got going the rest of the day?"

"Not a thing. What do you need?"

"I wanted you to drop me off at my lawyer's office this afternoon. Today we make it official and sign the papers for the Plaza Hotel and Suites."

"You don't need me to wait for you?"

"No, I'll call to find out where you are, and Alexis can drop me off there once we're done. Knowing her, she'll probably want to do something to celebrate."

"Okay, but you know you can call me and I'll come get you."

"I know. I'll call you regardless." Imani paused. "Was that Martel I heard when you came in?"

"It was."

"What's he talking about?"

"Nothing, but it sounds like he and Hareem are still on that Diamond thing."

Imani shook her head. "He said he was done with that. What were they talking about?"

"That Diamond can't keep her people safe and how that makes this the time to recruit her people."

"At least they're not plotting on going to war with her anymore. I've been trying to convince him that going to war and even the little shit he was doing to draw her out were bad for business. I thought I was getting through to him."

"You are getting through to him, Imani. Giving him control of the port gave him something more important and lucrative to focus on. Especially after he stole that big load on its way to Atlanta, but I guess we'll see."

"I guess we will."

Meanwhile, in the great room, Hareem thought about what Martel said and about Diamond being weak and this being the time to move on her. He'd known Martel long enough to know that he would much rather kill her and her people than talk, so he wondered sometimes if putting him in charge was the right play. Although he was confident that he could keep Martel in check, he knew that he needed to stay on top of him.

Just then, Hareem heard the front door open, and Mr. O came into the house with Loonie. When he found out that he had a granddaughter, Mr. O wanted to spend time with her and was quickly smitten with his grand-daughter and her mother as well. When he was in his room watching television, recovering from being shot, it was he, Loonie, and the baby. Eventually, he invited them to come live at the house, and Loonie, wanting what was best for her daughter and knowing that Mr. O would always take care of his granddaughter, accepted the invitation. Now, whenever he had a follow-up appointment, was going to see one of his lady friends, or had anywhere else that he had to go, he insisted that Loonie drive him.

Omeika heard her mother's voice and began to cry.

"Mommy's coming," Loonie said on her way to the great room to see about her daughter.

Hareem sat up when she came into the room, because despite the fact that he lived with Cynthia, he was still in love with Loonie and everything about her. He exhaled at the sight of her full breasts, small waist, and the way her ass looked when she bent over to pick up Omeika.

"Mommy's here, Omeika. Was Daddy watching sports on TV and ignoring his baby girl?"

"She went into her routine as soon as she heard your voice. Before that she was quiet. She didn't even scream when she saw Martel."

"Really? Maybe she's getting used to him."

"Maybe," Hareem said and thought about how he had told Martel to handle Winder and anybody else who was dissatisfied.

"Don't kill them. Recruit them. That's how you take over her business without firing a shot."

"Much easier to just kill them all," was Martel's chilling answer.

All Hareem could do was hope that he actually could keep his murderous friend in check.

Chapter Thirteen

Winder was standing behind the police barricade when they brought Ross's and Gail's bodies out of their apartment. When the coroner's truck left the scene, he walked away, taking out his phone.

"Sup?" Cameron answered, still asleep.

"Ross and Gail are dead."

Cameron sat up in bed and shielded his eyes from the sun. "Wait, what you say?"

"I said that somebody killed Ross and Gail."

"When?"

"Last night!" Winder shouted.

"Okay, nigga, you ain't gotta yell. It's too early for all that hollering. You know who did it?"

"No, but I know that Hareem is behind it, and I'm gonna kill that nigga."

"Okay, nigga, calm down. I'm gonna call Diamond, and I'll call you back."

"I'm telling you now, that bitch didn't wanna do shit when them niggas killed Hedrick, and I kept my mouth shut, but not this time. She don't wanna do shit, fuck her. I'll handle the shit myself."

"Let me talk to Diamond, and I'll call you back," Cameron repeated and hung up.

That was earlier that morning. It was now late in the day. Cameron had spoken with Diamond, and she told him some bullshit about how it didn't make sense that Hareem would have them killed and leave the product and $10,000 in cash for the cops to find.

"Fuck that dumb-ass shit that bitch talking. Could have been a hundred reasons why they didn't take the money and the dope. That bitch is weak, simple, and plain, and that's why she don't wanna retaliate for Ross and Gail."

He and his crew had piled into a car and were headed to one of the corners where Hareem's man, Devonte, did business. Ross had been murdered along with Gail. Winder didn't know exactly who killed them, but since they'd been having problems with Hareem and his people, to Winder it was natural to assume that they were involved in some way. They had business to take care of, and they were on their way to getting it done. Fuck what Diamond wanted.

"Hedrick was her muscle. But now he's dead."

Winder was in the back seat, his boy, Adler, was up front, and his cousin, Huxley, was driving the car. As they approached the corner, Winder could see Devonte and five of his men on the corner. He and Adler were both armed with AK47s and prepared their weapons as they came up on the corner.

"Roll on them!" Winder shouted, and as Huxley drove past the corner, he and Adler began shooting.

Two of Devonte's men were hit with semiautomatic gunfire right away, and they went down. He and the others scattered, reaching for their guns to shoot back. Devonte returned fire with a .45, while the other three shot back with 9 mms. Winder and Adler kept firing, but Devonte's men had taken cover, and now they were taking heavy fire.

"Go!" Winder yelled, and Huxley stepped on the gas, and Devonte's men came up firing as they sped away.

Alexis was at their lawyer's office with Imani when she got the text message from Cameron.

Winder did a drive-by on Devonte.

"Damn it," she said softly.

"Is everything all right?" their lawyer asked.

"Yes, but I need to go, so can we wrap this up?" she asked calmly, but on the inside, Alexis was fuming. She knew something like that was going to happen, but she had hoped Cameron would be able to contain Winder.

"We're just about done here," their lawyer said, and Imani leaned close to Alexis.

"Everything all right?"

"Yes. I just have something that I need to run back to the office to handle."

"Okay," Imani said, and they went on and finished their business with the lawyer.

Once that was concluded and the deal was final, Imani told Alexis to go on and leave. She would call Brock, and he would come to pick her up.

"You sure?"

"Yes. I told Brock I would call him. He doesn't mind coming to get me."

"You sure?" Alexis asked on her way to the door.

Imani sat down in the lobby and took out her phone. "Yes, Alexis. Brock can't get enough of me." She giggled and pointed toward the door. "Go on and do what you gotta do and call me later."

"We need to celebrate."

"We do."

"Thanks for understanding."

Imani pointed toward the door. "Go!"

"I'm going, I'm going," Alexis said and left the office.

She drove straight to the condo to change into something more appropriate for her Diamond persona. On the way there, Alexis called Cameron. Her first thought was to have him find Winder and bring him somewhere so she could deal with him. But then she thought better of it.

"What's up, Diamond?" Cameron answered when she called.

"Meet me at the condo," was all Alexis said, and then she ended the call. When he got there, Alexis opened the door and let him in.

"What's up, Diamond?"

Alexis said nothing. She shut and locked the door, and then she went and sat down in the living room. Cameron followed her in and then stood there.

"You want something to drink?" she asked after a while.

"Yes."

"Help yourself. You know where everything is."

Cameron went into the kitchen to get a glass and some ice before walking toward the bar in the corner of her living room. With his eyes on Alexis, trying to gauge her mood, he picked a bottle of Seagram's whiskey, poured a drink, and sat down across from Alexis.

"Maybe I wasn't clear, so let me ask. What did you and I talk about in this room a couple of hours ago?"

Cameron turned up his glass and finished it. He put the glass down. "About Ross getting killed and Winder thinking that it was Hareem who was behind it."

"That's what I thought you and I talked about." Alexis nodded her head and leaned forward. "And what was the conclusion that you and I came to?"

"That it wasn't Hareem, Martel, and them because they wouldn't have left the place dirty for the cops to find." He leaned forward quickly. "I explained all that to Winder and that it might have been some of their personal shit and we need to be sure before we do anything. He was cool about it. He said that he knew for a fact that Gail was fuckin' some nigga named Bauta, or some shit like that, and said he was gonna check him out."

"But he didn't check him out, did he?"

"No. He went straight to Devonte's corner and started shooting."

"Drive-by." Alexis shook her head. "Is Devonte dead?"

"No."

"Did they hit anybody?"

"I don't know."

Alexis clapped her hands. "And that is why drive-bys are inefficient."

"You been saying that for a long time."

There was silence in the room as Alexis looked at Cameron.

"You know whose fault this is?" she asked and then answered her own question. "This is your fault, Cam. Between you and Maxi, y'all need to deal with this." Alexis got up and stood over him. "Or would you rather I deal with him myself? Because if I have to deal with it, I'm gonna start with you and work my way down to him."

Alexis got quiet.

"Give me your gun," she said with her hand out.

Cameron reached behind his back and handed Alexis his gun.

"Get on your knees."

Cameron got off the couch and got on his knees. She made sure that there was one in the chamber before she put it to his head.

"Maybe I didn't make my wishes clear, so this time, I'm gonna say it so you understand, and you can make it clear to everybody else. Are you listening?"

"Yes."

"When I wanna start a war with Hareem, I will do something more effective than a damn drive-by. Do you understand me?"

"Yes, Diamond."

She handed him back his gun.

"Get up."

While Cameron got off the floor, Alexis went to sit down and crossed her legs.

"You let Maxi deal with Winder. I need you to do two things for me."

"What's that?"

"I need you to make sure we're ready when Martel hits back. And you know Martel is gonna hit back."

"What's the other?"

"Try to stop Martel from hitting back. Sit down with him if you have to, but let's try not to get into a shooting war with the gunrunner's little brother. Does that make sense to you?"

Cameron chuckled. "It does."

"Cam, I need you to do that for me, for us. When Hedrick was murdered, you told me you were ready, and I believed you."

"I am ready." Cameron stood. "I'll take care of this for you, Diamond." He picked up his glass, took it to the kitchen, and then walked to the door.

"Cameron."

When he looked back, Alexis was pointing her gun at him.

"Take care of this for me, or I will kill you and find somebody who can."

Cameron nodded and left the condo. When the door closed, Alexis put the gun down and picked up her phone.

"Hello."

"Hey, Imani. I took care of my business. You still wanna go somewhere to celebrate?"

"I sure do."

"Great. I'll swing by and pick you up around eight."

"See you then."

Alexis put her phone down and got up so she could change into something appropriate for her real estate agent, girlfriend/partner persona.

Chapter Fourteen

Celebration!

Alexis and Imani had lobster frittatas, eight-ounce center-cut filet mignon with white cheddar hash browns, and smoked salmon and caviar for dinner at the Capital Grille, and then they did a little bar hopping. Alexis dropped her off at her house at a little after one in the morning.

On the way to the house, Alexis and Imani were talking about their next potential project, St. Johns Square, a retail submarket located near Roosevelt Boulevard that offered easy access to the city's interstate system.

"The front of the property is well-lit and has pole signage and a rear parking area. It has security cameras already in place, and it has an excellent mix of tenants," Alexis said.

"What's the asking?"

"It's $1.3 million. That comes out to about one hundred and twelve dollars per square foot."

Imani laughed. "Did you do that math in your head?"

"No, I remembered it from the executive summary."

"Do you remember what the ratio of the property's net income to its purchase price was?"

"I'm not sure, but I think it said that the capitalization rate was around seven or eight percent. I have the summary at the house. I could check it out when we get there, but first I need to use the bathroom," Alexis said, and she drove faster.

When they made it to the house and went inside, Alexis rushed to the bathroom, while Imani went to the office to get the executive summary so they could talk more about it. Once she was finished in the bathroom, Alexis went to the great room to wait. While she was waiting for Imani, Alexis thought about the situation with Byron Ross and Gail Hopkins. She had told Cameron that she didn't think Hareem and Martel had anything to do with it because of the police confiscation.

She had known them for years and knew that Gail's occasional bouts of infidelity used to drive Ross crazy. Alexis thought that Cameron maybe was right. It may have been over some of their personal business and not what Hareem and Martel were doing.

But suppose she was wrong and they did have something to do with it?

Just then, she heard the front door open and close, and then Alexis heard laughter.

"Go ahead and run, nigga!" Martel said and laughed loudly. "Hope you make it without pissing on yourself," he said as he staggered into the great room and saw Alexis sitting there. From the first day that Martel came to see Hareem and Hareem introduced him to Alexis, he'd been deep into her and wished for the day when she would give in to one of his many lewd sexual advances toward her.

"Hello, Martel." Alexis could tell by the way he was walking that he was drunk.

"There she is!" Martel stumbled toward the couch and almost fell on his face. "My fantasy woman!"

"I am not your fantasy woman, Martel." Alexis was disgusted and a little frightened by the sight of him coming at her like that, and she wondered what he would do.

He plopped down on the couch next to her. "Come here. Give your fantasy man a kiss." Martel reached for Alexis, but she bounced up from the couch.

"Stop it, Martel!"

"Come on now," he slurred and got up. "Don't be like that," he said, coming toward her with his arms out. "Gimme a kiss."

Martel lunged for her, but Alexis moved out of the way quickly, and he almost fell again.

"I said stop it!" Alexis said loudly as she backed away from him.

"Okay, okay, I'll stop," Martel said, but he kept coming toward Alexis and eventually backed her into a corner. Alexis looked around for something to hit him with if it came to that. "I just wanna know when you gonna make a nigga's dreams come true and ride my face."

"You're disgusting."

"Am I interrupting something?" Imani said when she came into the great room and saw what was happening.

"Yes," Alexis said, and she moved around Martel.

"Thought so," Imani said as Hareem came into the great room.

"You ready to get outta here, Marty-mar?"

"Yeah, I'm ready." Martel looked at Alexis, and he laughed loud and hearty. "Did everything come out all right?" he asked, winking at Alexis while he moved toward the door.

"Whatever, nigga. How you doing, Alexis?"

"I'm fine, Hareem, but you need to teach your boy here some manners and how to talk to a woman."

"What you do, Marty-mar?"

"I didn't do nothing," he said and walked out of the great room with Hareem. "All I did was ask her for some pussy," Martel said and closed the front door behind him.

"He is so vulgar and crass," Imani said. "He's gross and obnoxious, too."

"He makes my flesh crawl every time I see him," Alexis said. "And then he opens his mouth and says something to disgust me."

"What did he say to you this time?"

"He called me his fantasy woman and wanted me to kiss him."

Imani frowned. "Yuck."

"I know, right. Then he asked me when I was going to make his dreams come true and ride his face."

"Disgusting."

"If you hadn't come into the room when you did, there was no telling what he might have done. You saw how drunk he was."

"I saw he had you pinned in the corner." Imani sat down and Alexis joined her. "You don't think that he was gonna try to rape you, do you?"

"Ain't no telling what his drunk ass was gonna do to me."

"I'll talk to Hareem about it."

"No need. I can handle Martel." She laughed. "At least, I can handle him when he's sober. Then he's just tactless, insensitive, and gross."

"Tactless, insensitive, and gross." Imani laughed. "That's most men."

"True." Alexis paused. "So, let's get back to the executive summary."

"Yes," Imani said, handing Alexis the binder that she was carrying.

Chapter Fifteen

After she left Imani's house and put her ordeal with Martel behind her, Alexis drove to her condo and transformed herself once again. When she was dressed, she got in the Jaguar and drove to Cameron's apartment.

"What's up, Diamond?"

"What's up, Cam?"

"Come in."

"I'm not staying long," Alexis said as she stepped inside the apartment.

When she got into the living room, two women were sitting on the couch. One was in a pair of Kobi Halperin Syd high-rise flare pants and a Fleur du Mal lily-embroidered long-lined triangle bra. The other only had an Ena Pelly Riri cut-out top on. They smiled and waved to Alexis, and she nodded.

"I just want to know what happened with Winder."

"I held a gun to his head, and Maxwell broke his little finger with a sledgehammer. Then I assured him that if he ever defied your wishes again, I would break the entire hand. After that, Winder assured me that nothing like that will ever happen again."

"I expected no less."

"I know that you didn't."

"Good night, Cam. I'll let you get back to what you were doing," Alexis said and turned to leave. Cameron's guests smiled and waved goodbye to Alexis, and she went home.

The following morning, Alexis was still tired and truly not feeling the day that she had in front of her. Both she and Imani had done their share of celebration drinking the night before, and she had just a bit of a headache. Alexis silenced the alarm, pulled the sheet over her head, and went back to sleep. When she woke up again after ten, Alexis began her day.

Before heading out, Alexis checked her email and schedule to confirm every client meeting that she had that day. She arrived at her first appointment twenty minutes early to make observations, take pictures, and review her property research. When the clients arrived, Alexis gave them an overview of the home and showed them around. She gave the buyers space to freely explore the home, but she stayed close enough to answer their questions.

"We love it."

Since her clients wanted to move forward with the sale, Alexis walked them through the offer process, and then she discussed their options with them, initiated the next steps, and connected them with a lender she trusted. After completing her showings for the day, Alexis headed to the office to wrap up for the day. She sent out buyer brokerage agreements to new clients to confirm representation, and then she did a final check of her email and her schedule for the following day. She was ready to head out and enjoy the rest of the night, maybe get some rest, so she could do it all over again the next day when her phone rang.

"South Jacksonville Realty, my name is Alexis Fox. How can I help you this evening?"

"Evening, Alexis."

"Evening, Horace."

"We need to talk," Detective Blakey said.

"The usual spot?"

"No. I haven't eaten all day, and I'm hungry."

"Tell me when and where, and I'll meet you," Alexis said.

"Why don't you meet me at the Stoner's Pizza Joint on Old St. Augustine Road?"

"Only if you buy me a slice. I haven't eaten all day either, and I'm starving."

"See you in an hour?"

"See you then."

An hour later, Alexis pulled her Avalon Hybrid into the parking lot at Stoner's Pizza Joint. She looked around for Blakey's car, and once she saw it, she got out and got in the car with him. He handed her a slice of pizza.

"You still like the Italian steak?"

"You remembered," Alexis said of the slice that was topped with steak, onions, mushrooms, green peppers, and mozzarella cheese. "What are you having?" she asked and took a bite of her slice.

"The No Brainer Deluxe with Italian sausage, ham, pepperoni, onions, green peppers, mushrooms, and mozzarella."

"That sounds good," she said with her mouth full of pizza.

"I'll order you one next time," he promised, and the two ate their slices in silence.

"So, what's going on, Horace?" Alexis asked when she was just about finished with her slice.

Horace took the last bite of his No Brainer slice and wiped his mouth. "There was a shooting in broad daylight yesterday at the corner of Liberty and Eighth Street. Do you know anything about that?"

"Unfortunately, I do."

"Two people are dead, Alexis. And did I mention that it was in broad daylight?"

"You did, and I've received assurances that nothing like that will ever happen again."

"Make sure."

"I will." Alexis finished her slice. "You heard anything new to report about Hedrick's murder?" She had decided that if the investigation came too close to Brock, she would tell Imani, even if it meant that Alexis would have to tell the truth about her secret life as Diamond.

"I have nothing new."

"What about the murders of Byron Ross and Gail Hopkins?"

"That's not my case, but I will look into it for you and let you know something tomorrow. I did follow up on that name you gave me: Bauta." He shook his head. "Nothing. I can't even say if it's a real person because none of the usual suspects have ever heard of him. More details about who he is or maybe even a last name would help."

"If I get more, I'll let you know." Alexis paused. "Do I have any exposure on the Liberty drive-by?"

"Have them ditch the car. There are some cameras in that area."

"I'll have Maxwell take care of it. Anything else?"

"There is." Blakey pulled another No Brainer slice out of the bag. "I'm a little concerned about what I've been hearing in the streets."

"What are you hearing?"

"That some of Hedrick's old crew are dissatisfied with the way you're treating them."

Alexis shook her head in disgust. "Winder," she spit out.

"They feel disrespected." Blakey took another bite.

"He's the one responsible for the shooting at Liberty."

"I figured as much."

"Don't worry," she said.

"Who said I was worried? I'm concerned. There's a difference."

"Well, don't be concerned. I have Maxwell taking care of the problem, and as I said, I've received assurances."

"I know that Hedrick did a lot for you and he's gonna be hard to replace, but you need to get on top of this before it becomes something that I can't handle for you."

"I'm on it," Alexis said, reaching into her Kate Spade New York Hudson flap shoulder bag and taking out an envelope. She handed it to Blakey.

"Be careful."

"Always."

After meeting with him, Alexis was tired and thought about going home for the night, but she knew that she needed to check on Cameron and Maxwell. Therefore, she drove to the condo and changed her clothes.

As she laid out the clothes that she was going to put on, her personal phone rang. Alexis picked up the cell and looked at the display. She smiled when she saw who was calling.

"Hey, you," she answered.

"How are you, Alexis?"

"I'm wonderful, Ronan."

His name was Ronan Goddard, and he was a lawyer who Alexis met while she was waiting in line to order her food at Firehouse Subs. By that time, Bells had been dead for a couple of years, and she was just starting to get back into the dating world.

"How are you?" Alexis asked.

"I'm fine. I'm in town for a couple of days, and I wanted to know, are you free tomorrow for dinner?"

"I am free, and I would love to have dinner with you," Alexis said, going into her closet and coming out with a pair of Tom Ford leather platform peep-toe pumps.

He chuckled. "You still work late every night?"

"Every night. At the office wrapping up for the night as we speak," she lied.

"So what time is good for you?"

"Let's say eight o'clock."

"Sounds good."

"Text me the details, and I will see you tomorrow."

"Looking forward to it."

"So am I. Good night," Alexis said, and then she got dressed to go meet Cameron.

Chapter Sixteen

Eight of Hareem's men were at Chub's apartment when he arrived with Martel.

"What happened?" Hareem asked.

"We were at the spot, doing our thing," Devonte began. "Then I see this car rolling up on us slowly." He paused for effect and looked around the room. "I see this nigga Adler in the front seat, and I'm not sure, but I think it was that nigga Winder in the back. Then I saw the guns come out."

"If it was Winder and Adler, you know Huxley was with them," Chub added.

Martel looked at Hareem. Although he had handed power to Martel, two of his men—two of his friends— were dead. They had all come up from Miami together. They were like a family.

"What you wanna do?" Martel asked.

"Let's get them," Hareem said, and his men all bounced to their feet. "Where the fuck y'all going?"

"You said let's get them," Jarell said.

"Where you going?" Hareem looked around the room. "Who y'all going after?"

He looked around the room at his men. Nobody said a word.

"That's what I thought. That's the problem: too many niggas running out doing shit without a plan. That's how shit gets fucked up and niggas get killed. Now sit the fuck down and let's plan how we gonna do this."

***

The following night, Devonte, Jamarcus, Chub, and Jarell were parked outside the house where they were told Adler and Huxley could be found. Jarell went to have a look.

"There's four of them in there," he reported.

Jamarcus nodded and went to the trunk and opened it. He reached in and picked up the ML37 grenade launcher and handed it to Chub.

"What's this?"

"That, my friend, is the ML37 grenade launcher."

"Sweet."

He put his arm around Chub's shoulder. "A little present from Hareem."

Chub looked at the weapon and ran his hand across it. "Shit," he said excitedly and aimed it.

Jamarcus moved the barrel and pointed it toward the house. "When we get set, you fire."

"Bet!"

When Devonte and Jamarcus were in place, Chub fired a flash-bang grenade into the house, and Devonte and Jamarcus went in. The sudden flash of light and loud noise distracted the three men. Devonte came in blasting and shot one man as he came out of the kitchen. Adler was on the couch. Jamarcus hit him with his first two shots before he could get a shot off. He stood over him and fired two more shots to Adler's head.

One of Winder's men was at the back door. He came charging down the hall when he heard the shots fired. Jamarcus fired two shots to his chest and then one to the head. Just then, Huxley ran into the room and fired at Devonte and then ran into the bedroom. Devonte went after him, while Jamarcus ran to the front door. Devonte heard a window breaking, and then he heard two shots. He went to the window, and when he got outside, he saw that Chub was down. Huxley had Jamarcus pinned down on the porch as he kept firing and made his way to his car.

When Devonte began firing at Huxley, it gave Jamarcus time to get to his feet and reload his gun. Devonte went to check on Chub.

"I'll be all right," he said as Huxley made it to his car, got in, and drove off.

Jamarcus ran behind the car, firing shots until his gun was empty. Devonte pulled up alongside him.

"Get in!"

Devonte went down the street after Huxley. Jamarcus opened fire at the car until the clip was empty. Devonte handed him another gun, and he resumed firing. One of his shots hit Huxley's back tire, and he slammed into some parked cars. He was shaken up, but he got out of the car and took a couple of shots at Devonte and Jamarcus when they got out of the car.

When they returned fire, Huxley ran down the street. Jamarcus got back in the car, while Devonte ran after him. Huxley ducked behind a truck and began firing at Devonte. Devonte hit the ground and fired back. When Huxley stopped, turned around quickly, and fired a couple of shots, Devonte dove for cover behind a car as the bullets ricocheted off the windshield.

When he ran, Devonte jumped up and took off behind him. Huxley looked over his shoulder and could see that Devonte was catching up to him, so he turned around quickly and fired. Devonte was pinned down while Huxley kept firing until he emptied the clip and started running again. Devonte got up and quickly got off a couple of shots at Huxley but missed him.

By the time Devonte reached the corner, Huxley was nowhere in sight. He looked around.

"There that muthafucka go."

Devonte watched Huxley go inside a bar. He put the silencer on his gun and then went in after him. Huxley peeked out the window, and when he didn't see Devonte or Jamarcus, he headed for the bar.

"Dewar's straight up. Make it a double."

When the bartender returned with his drink, Huxley paid him and drank it down. He was about to signal for another when he felt pressure in the small of his back.

"Now we gonna walk up outta here nice and quiet," Devonte said and pushed his gun a little harder into Huxley's back.

Huxley put down his glass, and Devonte walked him out of the bar. He kept the barrel to his back as they went down the street and around the corner, and then they went into an alley. Devonte pushed Huxley, and he stumbled to the ground. He scrambled to his knees, held his hands up in front of his face, and begged for his life.

"Please don't kill me! I just drove the car! I didn't kill nobody!"

Devonte shot Huxley three times in the head.

Chapter Seventeen

At seven forty-five, Alexis pulled into the parking lot at Rue Saint-Marc, a modern French bistro-style bar with an outdoor patio that served French-inspired cuisine in the San Marco neighborhood of Jacksonville, to meet Ronan Goddard for dinner.

"I'm not your average thirty-one flavors," was what Alexis once said of herself.

When they first met, she told him that her world was complicated, and, thinking that what complicated her world was another man, he told her that he was up to the challenge and could deal with whatever she had going on. Their second date was interrupted when Hedrick called. Their third date ended with them having sex for the first time. It was amazing. After that, Alexis tried to maintain a relationship with Ronan, but it wasn't to be.

After a while, Ronan began to question where she ran off to when she got those late-night calls. Even though he said that he could deal with it, he began to believe that she was seeing somebody else. When he confronted her about it, Alexis assured him that she wasn't seeing anybody else, and then she reminded him that she told him that her world was complicated.

However, after a while, when her behavior didn't change, her denials meant little, and he was sure that there was somebody else. Where in the beginning Ronan didn't care if she had somebody else because he just wanted to fuck her, now that he had developed feelings for her, he wanted to know who it was. His jealousy and constant accusations as well as her double life were what broke them.

"Alexis Fox. I have a reservation."

"Yes, right this way, Ms. Fox."

Alexis followed the hostess to the table where Ronan was waiting. He stood up when he saw her coming. He was wearing a plaid Canali Milano suit and wearing it well. Ronan smiled that smile that used to make her wet.

"How are you, Alexis?" He gave her a hug that reminded her of the nights in his arms making love.

"I'm wonderful, Ronan. How are you?"

"I'm doing great." He pulled her chair out for her. "You look amazing."

That night, Alexis was wearing a tangerine Lela Rose draped textured crepe sheath dress that sent chills up and down his spine and made him wonder why he broke it off with her and moved to Houston.

Because she was fucking somebody behind your back, that's why, he reminded himself. Ronan looked at Alexis as she sat down. Fine as she was, did that really matter? He asked himself about it in retrospect and sat down across from her.

"It is so good to see you," she said, reaching across the table and taking his hands in hers. The warmth of her hands made his length twitch. "So, what brings you to Jacksonville?"

"I'm in town for the American Immigration Lawyers Association Annual Conference on Immigration Law at the Ritz-Carlton in Amelia Island," he said as their server arrived at the table.

"Can I start you off with something from the bar?"

"Yes," Ronan said. "A bottle of your best champagne."

"Veuve Clicquot, an excellent choice," their server said, and once he had taken their order, he left the ex-lovers alone.

The Rue Experience with Wine Pairings boasted of a three-course prix fixe menu with the chef's presentation of the season's best ingredients. The first course was A.B. Urban Farms lettuce with apples, pecans, pecorino, and cider vinaigrette. Mayport shrimp was served with black truffle polenta, artichoke, guanciale, and hazelnut vinaigrette. Their second course featured Atlantic halibut, prepared with speck ham and parsley root, and Painted Hills bavette steak served with wild nettle puree, farro piccolo, lion's mane mushrooms, confit shallot, and bordelaise. For the third dessert course, the ex-lovers had Chocolate Delice, a salted caramel Anjou pear, and hazelnut-praline ice cream.

"How have you been doing, Alexis?"

"Things are going great for me. Do you remember my friend Imani?"

Ronan nodded. "The one in the shipping business?" Ronan remembered thinking that they were lovers because of the amount of time that Alexis used Imani as an excuse to get away. When Alexis finally did introduce him to Imani, Ronan wished that if they were lovers, they would invite him to join them when they had sex.

"That's her."

"How is she?" he asked and braced himself for her answer, half expecting her to say that she and Imani were married or something like that.

"She's doing great. She and I went into business together, and now we own two properties: The Park at Atlantic Beach, which we're converting into condominiums, and we just closed on and plan to renovate the Plaza Hotel and Suites."

"That's excellent."

"What about you? How have you been? How's Houston treating you?"

As his relationship with Alexis continued to deterio-
rate, Ronan had been interviewed and was hired by Cary,
Estrada, Walsh & Associates.

"Houston is great. I love it there."

"And the job?"

"I can actually say that I love what I do, and it's not just
the money, which is excellent."

"So, you're practicing immigration law now?"

"No, that's just another feather in my cap. I am very
happy being the worst type of corporate shark." Ronan
chuckled. "Sometimes it gets a little lonely, but overall,
things are good." He sipped his cocktail. "I'm on track to
make partner."

"That's great. I am so happy for you." Alexis wiped her
mouth and put down her napkin. "What did you mean,
sometimes it gets lonely?"

"Most days, at most of the meetings I go to," he said, "I
am the only black man in the room." He chuckled. "And
all of my clients are white."

"I see."

"I'm what they call the diversity hire at the firm. I call
myself the spook who sat by the door." Ronan chuckled,
referring to the 1973 film *The Spook Who Sat by the
Door,* the fictional story of the first black CIA officer. "I
am the only black man at the firm. Oh, there are three
black women who work there. One is a receptionist, one
is an admin, and one is a legal clerk."

It was then that Alexis's cell rang, and Ronan got a
look on his face as his mind flashed back to the days
when Alexis would have to drop everything and leave just
about every time her phone rang. She knew that it was
Cameron calling.

"I need to take this." She got up from the table to take
the call. "What's up?"

"Hareem hit back," Cameron informed. "Adler and Huxley are dead."

"I'm on my way," Alexis said and returned to the table with Ronan.

"Is everything all right?" he asked when she sat down.

"No. Something came up suddenly at one of my properties, and I have to take care of it."

"I understand," Ronan said even though he didn't understand at all. This was just more of the same for Alexis, and it only served to reaffirm his reason for ending it and moving to Houston.

"I'm sorry," Alexis said as she gathered her things to leave.

"I guess some things never change."

Alexis paused, looked at Ronan, and thought about what he said. She remembered how they'd fought constantly about her always having to leave and how the double life that she was living ruined the relationship.

Alexis held up one finger. She picked up her cell and called Cameron back.

"What's up?"

"Deal with the situation, and I'll call you in the morning," Alexis said and ended the call without waiting for Cameron to respond. Then she made a big show of turning off her phone and placing it back in her Chiara Boni Elena leather chain-strap clutch. "Now, you were saying?"

Ronan chuckled and shook his head. "That maybe some things do change."

"And some things don't." Alexis leaned forward and took his hand in hers. It had the same effect that it did the last time she touched him. "What hotel did you say you were staying at?"

"The Ritz-Carlton on Amelia Island."

Alexis purred. "That's right."

"You remember, I'm here for the conference on immigration law."

"At the Ritz-Carlton." Alexis leaned forward and ran
her tongue across her lips. "On Amelia Island."

"That's right," Ronan said, smiling broadly.

"I've never been to the Ritz-Carlton." Alexis paused
while she stared into his eyes. "On Amelia Island."

Ronan squeezed her hands. "I would love to show you
the view from the ocean suite."

"I'll follow you."

"Check!"

His hands were all over her body as soon as they closed
the door. They went from her breasts to her hips and her
ass and back up to her breasts again. He kissed her again,
nibbled her chin, and sucked her neck. Their foreplay
was fiery and sweet, and her body responded. It made her
even wetter and more eager to have him inside of her.

Ronan reached behind her back and unhooked her bra
as he continued to finger her slit through her panties.
The sensation sent wave after wave of delicious pleasure
through her body, and her body shook with anticipation.
He eased Alexis out of her dress and then tossed it across
the room. Once her breasts were free, Ronan took one of
Alexis's nipples into his mouth, teased it, and sucked it.
The way his lips wrapped around her hard nipple made
her toes curl.

"I missed you," Alexis breathlessly admitted. *Damn, it
feels so good. He feels so good, so right.*

Ronan pushed her legs open with one hand and dipped
his finger into her. Alexis closed her eyes, and she felt
her body tremble as his penetrating finger eased in and
out of her. She bit her bottom lip to stop herself from
screaming. He buried his head deep between her thighs,

sucked her clit, and fingered her. It caused her spine to arch and her hands to hold him tightly.

"Oh, Ronan," Alexis whispered, aching for more as desire radiated throughout her body.

Then he spread her lips while squeezing her breast and made small circles around her clit with the tip of his tongue. He slid his tongue inside of her, sucked her lips, and felt her body quiver as her thighs pressed together and her body convulsed.

The feeling was so intense and centered that she lost her train of thought. Alexis kissed him passionately, lying on the bed, and her legs spread open as if she were inviting him in. She stroked his now-massive erection, and she remembered how empty she felt when he told her he was taking that dick to Houston.

You never forget being loved like that, so right, so perfect, and he was giving it to her just the way Alexis needed.

She didn't know when any of this would happen again and wanted to enjoy the sensation and savor it. The sensation started to radiate out, and Alexis exploded, screaming.

Ronan pulled her on top of him, and Alexis wiggled her hips and moved her body slowly until she had adjusted herself to his size. She was caught up in the rapture of how good he felt inside her. They were, once again, making love like they were made for each other. It caused her to remember how magnificently in tune with each other's bodies they once were. That was how it used to be between them. Alexis could feel the tension simmering within her. Each thunderous stroke was so intense that she'd immediately tighten around him.

"I'm cumming!" she yelled, and her head drifted back.

They both passed out for a while but woke up shortly thereafter. Alexis lay there for a while, basking in the moment, and then she got out of bed and headed toward the bathroom. When he heard the shower come on, Ronan propped a pillow behind his head.

"I guess some things never change."

Alexis was dressed when she came out of the bathroom. "I had fun." She went to the bed and kissed Ronan on the cheek.

"I did too."

"Call me next time you're in the city."

A dejected Ronan nodded. Although he refused to admit it to himself, there was a part of him that came to Jacksonville to convince Alexis to think about moving to Houston. He loved her, and the passage of time and the distance between them had done little to change that. Ronan started to tell her that he would be in the city for another week, but what would be the point?

Ronan watched Alexis as she left the suite and knew that she would never change, and it was futile to believe that she would.

As she walked down the hall toward the elevator, Alexis took out her cell and made a call.

"What's up, Diamond?" Cameron asked.

"Where are you?"

"I'm at Huxley's woman's house."

"Stay there. I'm on my way."

Chapter Eighteen

The following day, Alexis stood in her closet, swaying back and forth to the music in her mind as she tried to decide what to wear. Once she had made her selection, she came out of the closet and laid the Chiara Boni La Petite Robe Triana floral wrap dress that she planned to wear that day out on the bed and headed for the shower. Once it reached the perfect temperature, Alexis stepped in and let the water caress her body. As she slid the loofah over her skin, she thought about what she had to do when she got to the office, and then her mind drifted back to Cameron and the night before.

When she had arrived at Huxley's woman's house, he told her what he knew about Adler's and Huxley's deaths. Alexis was mad because this was all because Winder didn't listen. She told Cameron to do whatever he had to do to arrange a sit-down with Martel to make peace.

Once she was dressed, Alexis slipped on her Stuart Weitzman multicolored leather pumps, got in her Avalon Hybrid, and went to put in her work for another long day. After a stop at the Starbucks drive-through for a turkey bacon, cheddar, and egg white sandwich and grande cappuccino, she was in the office at seven thirty that morning. Her day began with a review of her schedule for the day, but as she responded to the emails that she received the day before, Alexis thought about Ronan and how good it was to see him. How good it felt to be in his arms again. She sat back in her chair, closed her eyes, and remembered the way Ronan kissed her as he led her toward the bed.

The illumination of the soft moonlight pouring through the curtains made his eyes look so beautiful, so inviting. He leaned forward and kissed her. She moved closer to him, and he put his arms around her, and they kissed again. Alexis enjoyed the feeling of sheer ecstasy as his hands explored her body. His nipples got harder, and his body ached to feel her tongue against them. Ronan's nipples were his weakness, and she knew it, and she had every intention of exploiting that fact.

Alexis opened her eyes and tried to focus on work, but she kept thinking about his tongue pushing its way into her mouth. The look in his eyes as he squeezed her breasts softly, caressing them, loving them with both of his hands. Then he took her nipple into his mouth and began sucking it greedily, rolling it around in his mouth. Then there was a knock at her door.

"How are you doing, Alexis?"

When Alexis looked up, Hareem was standing in her doorway, and it startled her.

"Hey, Hareem."

"I didn't mean to startle you."

"That's all right. I was too focused on these reports. What are you doing here?"

"I came to pick up Cynthia. Her car is in the shop, so I thought I'd stop in and say hello to you while I was here."

"I'm glad you did. Come in. Sit down," she said and thought about the irony.

The night before, she told Cameron to arrange a sit-down with Martel, and there she was, sitting down with Hareem. It occurred to her that if she chose to be honest, she could tell him that she was Diamond, and they could settle whatever differences they had.

"How have you been, and how is the baby? What's her name again?"

"Omeika."

"Omeika, that is such a pretty name."

"Like I said, I can't take any credit for that, but she's doing fine."

"That's good."

"I see you and Imani are doing big things."

"Yes. We just closed on the Plaza Hotel."

"So I hear, and she said she is on the hunt for the next property."

"Your sister is aggressive."

"No doubt about that."

Alexis paused for a second or two, and then she decided to go for it. "I'm glad you stopped by because there's something—"

At that second, Cynthia appeared at the office door. "I'm ready to go," she said, looked at Alexis, and rolled her eyes. "Let's get outta here."

"I've been waiting for you." Hareem sprang to his feet. "Good to see you, Alexis."

"Good to see you too," she said, and he left the office with Cynthia. Alexis exhaled and cursed at the opportunity lost. *Leave it to Cynthia to fuck it up,* she thought as her phone rang.

"South Jacksonville Realty, my name is Alexis Fox. How can I help you today?"

"Good morning, Alexis."

"Ronan." She exhaled, and suddenly her regrets about not coming clean with Hareem were gone, and all she could think about in that moment was his slow and constant pace, the way he slid in and out of her, making her feel every sensation that his length had to offer. The night before, he made love to her the way she wanted him to, the way she needed him to, the way she had to have it. "How are you doing this morning?"

"Doing fine." He cleared his throat. "I just called to apologize."

"Apologize? For what?"

"For being mad at you."

"Me? What were you mad at me for?" Alexis asked, unsure of what she had done, and she was confused about it. There she was thinking about how amazing the night before was, and he was mad about something.

"For being yourself." He paused. "I came here thinking that I would call you and you would drop everything and spend this time with me, and when that didn't happen, I was mad. And then I thought about it, and I had to ask myself, 'Why? Why am I mad at her? This is who she is.'"

"I'm sorry."

"No, don't apologize for being who you are." He chuckled. "I don't know what I was expecting."

"I don't know what to say other than I'm sorry." Alexis paused to think that this was how it used to be between them and how it was responsible for him moving to Houston. "How much longer are you going to be in Jacksonville?"

"Until next Monday."

"Next Monday?"

"Yes. Today is the first day of the conference."

"I don't know why, probably because I didn't ask, but I thought that your conference was over and you were leaving today."

"No. I came in a couple of days early—"

"To spend that time with me. I'm sorry."

"Don't be. It's my fault for thinking that you would just drop whatever you were doing to spend that time with me just because I showed up out of nowhere after all this time."

"I'm sorry."

"Stop saying that. You don't have to apologize for being yourself."

"But I feel so bad."

"Then make it up to me by having dinner with me tonight."

"I can't tonight. I have plans."

"Are you seeing somebody?" Ronan asked and held his breath in anticipation of her answer.

"No, I have a meeting with the subcontractor working on condo conversion at The Park at Atlantic," she lied quickly and easily.

"Tomorrow?"

"Meeting with Imani to inspect the Plaza Hotel."

"I understand. You're a busy woman, and I did just show up unannounced."

"It's not that I don't want to see you, because I do."

"Just not tonight."

"I didn't say that. What I have to do won't take me all night." Alexis paused. "So can I call you when my subcontractor meeting is over?"

"You sure can," Ronan said, and she could hear how much lighter his voice sounded.

"Awesome," she said as another call came in on the office phone. "I need to take this call, but I will see you tonight. Have a good day, and we'll talk later," Alexis said and took the call. "South Jacksonville Realty, my name is Alexis Fox. How can I help you today?"

When her workday at the office was over, Alexis turned off her computer and headed out for the night. She drove to her condo to change her clothes, and then she went to Cameron's apartment.

"Come in, Diamond," he said and held the door open for her to come in.

"Did you arrange a meeting with Martel?"

"I'm working on it."

"What does that mean?"

"That I reached out to Angela—"

"Angela?"

"Yeah, she and Loonie are first cousins. She's gonna meet Loonie tomorrow morning at the Denny's by the airport."

"Okay. Let me know how that goes," Alexis said, and once she was finished with Cameron, she left his apartment and went home.

After she had taken a bath and had a chance to unwind, Alexis called Ronan.

"Hello, Alexis."

"Are you busy?"

"No."

"I'm on my way."

"See you when you get here," Ronan said, and his mind flashed back to the days when he lived there, and they were together. Alexis would do him the same way, and it always made him feel as if he were nothing more than dick to her. Whether that was the case or not didn't matter. At least, it didn't then. He was in love with Alexis and would gladly take whatever time she had to offer.

They looked into each other's eyes when he opened the door and saw her standing there. He reached for her face and pulled her toward him. Their tongues became entangled in passion. Ronan took off his pants and then quickly unzipped her dress. He kissed her again, gently laid her body down on the bed, and they made love until Alexis screamed in ecstasy.

When their lovemaking was over, Ronan retreated to his side of the bed, breathing hard and shaking. He expected Alexis to get up and head for the shower, but instead, she rolled into his arms and fell asleep.

Chapter Nineteen

"Mommy's coming," Loonie said to Omeika, who was standing up in her playpen, screaming bloody murder while her mother got dressed to meet her cousin, Angela Hampton. They had seen each other at the funeral for Marques, and they promised to get together. She and Angela weren't really all that close, so Loonie thought it was just talk. Therefore, she was surprised to get Angela's call about meeting for breakfast.

Once she was dressed, Loonie gave Omeika a bath and got her dressed before she came downstairs. Kimberly was just finishing up cooking the feast that she prepared each morning. Most mornings, Imani and Brock showed up to eat, and Hareem came at least two or three times a week, sometimes with Cynthia, most times without. He came alone more now that Loonie was living there. But that morning, it was just Mr. O at the table when she came down.

"You should have invited her over here for breakfast," Mr. O commented as Loonie got a cup of coffee. She really liked Mr. O as much as he liked her. She had gotten tired of calling him Mr. O and referring to him as her daughter's grandfather, so she started calling him Pops. "The food is much better here than some fuckin' Denny's."

"Language around your granddaughter, Pops."

"Sorry. But the food is much better."

"You wanna come with me?"

"No," he said as Kimberly took the cup from Loonie's hand and poured it into a stainless-steel insulated coffee mug.

"Thank you, Kimberly. Don't worry, Pops. I'll be back in time to watch our shows."

At one time, the television in Mr. O's room while he was recovering would either be on ESPN or the NFL channel, and she, being a sports fan, would happily watch whatever was on and talk sports with him. Nowadays, Loonie had stretched their television viewing to include the judge shows, *Maury,* and *The View.*

"Who said I was worried?"

"Nobody," she said.

She got the keys to his Lexus LS 500 F Sport, which she always drove for him, and headed out for the Denny's by the airport. When she arrived at the restaurant and went inside, Loonie was surprised that her cousin Angela wasn't alone.

"Hey, Loonie," Angela said when she saw her and Omeika coming to the table.

"What's up with this, Angela?"

"This is Cameron. He works for Diamond," Angela replied.

"I know who the fuck he is. So, what is this? You here to kidnap me or some shit?" Loonie asked, regretting her decision to leave behind the gun Hareem insisted she needed. "You see I got the baby with me."

"No, cuz. Calm down. It ain't nothing like that."

"So, what the fuck is up then?" Loonie demanded to know. She was getting loud and attracting attention, but she didn't seem to care.

Cameron held his hands up. "I just need your help, that's all."

"Help? Help with what?"

"Sit down, Loonie," Angela said.

"Fuck that! Help with what?"

"I need to talk to Hareem to see if we can't settle our differences. And I need your help to arrange the sit-down. That's all I need."

"Oh," Loonie said and calmed down. "I can do that."

She sat down at the table with them just as the waitress arrived. Loonie had the Santa Fe Skillet and Angela ordered the Spicy Moons Over My Hammy breakfast sandwich. Cameron didn't stay for breakfast. Once Loonie agreed to set up the sit-down, he left Denny's.

"There are my girls," Hareem exclaimed when they came into the house.

"Good, you're here. I need to talk to you about something."

"What?"

"Let me get the baby settled first and I'll tell you," Loonie said and went upstairs to put Omeika down for a nap and to check on Mr. O.

"So, what did you wanna talk to me about?" Hareem asked when Loonie came back into the great room.

"I had breakfast this morning with my cousin, Angela."

"I heard."

"Cameron was there when I got there."

Hareem got mad and immediately thought the worst. "What was he doing there?"

"He wants to sit down with you to settle y'all's differences."

Hareem laughed. "'Niggas love to scream peace after they start some shit.'"

"'Pay attention,'" Loonie said, quoting the next line from 2Pac's classic, "When We Ride On Our Enemies."

"It's Cameron who wanna meet, not Diamond, right?"

"He didn't say nothing about Diamond. He said he need to talk to you about settling y'all's differences."

"Didn't think so."

"You don't think it's a trap, do you?"

"No. Marty-mar got her niggas on the run." He paused to think. "You tell Angela that Marty-mar will meet Cameron," Hareem said and felt like he had come a step closer to either bringing Diamond on board or driving her out of the market.

The following night, at a place called Netta's Food for the Soul, Cameron and Maxwell sat down with Martel and Chub to settle their differences. After which, Cameron called Alexis.

"It's done."

Chapter Twenty

Martel parked his truck in the parking lot at Popeyes on Soutel Drive and went inside. He stood there in line, looking at the menu. Martel loved their chicken and seafood, so he was a regular diner. He usually got the surf and turf combo or the five-piece tenders combo and a Coke, but that day he was in a good mood and was feeling like getting something a little different. When it was his turn in line, he stepped to the counter.

"Welcome to Popeyes, what can I get for you?"

"Let me have the popcorn shrimp combo, red beans and rice, and a biscuit."

"You want something to drink with that?"

"I'll have the chilled mango lemonade."

"This for here or to go?"

"That's gonna be for here."

Once Martel had paid for his meal, the cashier handed him his change and asked him to have a seat. She said that she would bring it out to him.

"Thank you, baby," he said when she handed him his change. "You must be new."

She leaned on the counter and smiled at Martel. "I just started yesterday."

"What's your name?"

"Chriscinda."

"That's a pretty name," he said and went to sit down.

When Chriscinda brought his food to the table and gave it to Martel, she included her phone number, and then she went back behind the counter with a promise that Martel would call her.

He was just about finished eating his red beans and rice when he saw Winder's car pull into the parking lot, and another car rolled in right behind it. He popped a shrimp in his mouth and watched as all eight doors on the two cars seemed to open at the same time. When Winder got out and all eight men started for Popeyes, Martel took out his gun and made sure one was in the chamber before he placed it on the table. He popped a shrimp in his mouth.

"What's up, Martel?" Winder said when he and his men came in and started for the table where he was sitting.

He put his hand on his gun. "I thought we would talk alone."

Winder motioned with his hand for his men to wait outside, and they turned to leave.

"I was gonna order something," Truevon said, and Winder pointed to the door. He stood shaking his head until his men had left before he sat down at the table with Martel.

"What happened to your hand?" Martel asked, looking at the cast on Winder's hand and little finger.

"This?" He held up his hand. "It ain't nothing. Had a little accident, no big deal." But it was a big deal. Winder's hand hurt like hell and throbbed every time he thought about the shit-eating grin on Maxwell's face when he hit him with the sledgehammer.

He looked at the gun and then at Martel. "What's up with that?"

"This?" he chuckled and pointed to the gun. Martel picked up and put away the gun. "So, what's up with you?"

"Came to see what you talking about."

"The way I hear it is that you ain't satisfied with the way Diamond is doing you."

"That's right. And I'm thinking about making a move, and if I like what I hear, it won't just be me making the move."

"How many niggas you talking about bringing with you?" Martel asked, looking out the window at the seven men who came with Winder, and he anxiously anticipated eventually bringing them all on board.

"Who and how many people I got with me don't concern you, at least not for the purposes of this conversation."

He nodded. "That's fair." Martel popped another shrimp in his mouth. "You get premium pricing, and you know we have the superior product. You call your own shots, and you handle the niggas who come with you any way you want."

"That's fair."

"More than." He popped a shrimp in his mouth and glanced at his gun. "Especially after Liberty."

Since he and Cameron had made peace, Winder was hoping that Martel wouldn't bring up the drive-by shooting.

"Yeah, well, Adler and Huxley are dead, so I figure that makes us even," Winder said, and Martel nodded and finished his mango lemonade.

"You heard what I had to say. Let me know what you wanna do."

Martel stood up, picked up his trash, and headed for the exit without another word because, as far as he was concerned, they were far from even. Once he got revenge for the two men he had lost in the Liberty drive-by, then, and only then, would they be even.

He stopped at the door. "What time you get off?" Martel asked Chriscinda.

"Nine o'clock."

"I'll call you," Martel said and walked out.

Chapter Twenty-one

Martel walked out of the Popeyes on Soutel Drive and went to his car. He sat there for a while and watched as Winder came out and approached his crew. When they got in their cars and drove away, Martel gave them a few seconds before he fell in behind them. He kept his distance and wasn't seen when they arrived at Winder's apartment complex. Martel parked a couple of buildings away where he had a good view, and then he watched Gatlin and Becket when they went inside with Winder.

"What you gonna do?" Beckett asked.

"About Martel? I don't know yet."

But he did. His hand still hurt from going against Diamond and defying her wishes, and at that moment, he wasn't interested in being in that position again. As far as he was concerned, for the time being, he wasn't going anywhere. But he was interested in Martel's offer. Although he understood why he didn't, Winder only wished he had gone into detail, especially about price. It would be a conversation that he was sure they would have in the future. Martel respected him as Hedrick's successor, which was more respect than Diamond showed him.

Just then, the doorbell rang, and Winder went to see who it was.

"But I need you and Gatlin to go by and see Andre and Butch to collect the money they owe just in case I decide to make that move."

"You got it," Becket said, and Winder opened the door.

"Hey, Perry," Eliza said, caressing his face as she walked into the apartment with two of her dick-sucking crackhead friends.

"What's up, Eliza?"

"Nothing much. This is my friend Kalisha, and this is Chantelle," Eliza said as they came into the apartment.

"How you ladies doing?" Winder asked and then looked at Becket and Gatlin. "What y'all waiting for?"

"Nothing," Becket said, looking at Eliza looking at him, and smiling. "We gone," he said and left the apartment with Gatlin.

As soon as they shut the door and had made their way down the steps, Gatlin burst out laughing his ass off.

"That nigga scared to fucking death of Diamond," Gatlin said as they walked to the car.

"I know." Becket laughed. "That hand is killing him. Your boy there don't want no more of fuckin' with Diamond."

"I know that's right. That nigga ain't going no-damn-where," Gatlin said as they got in the car.

"Talking about he ain't decided. Bullshit!" Becket laughed, and he started the car. "That nigga don't wanna see Cam and Maxwell at his door no more in life," he said, and they drove right past Martel. He smiled, shook his head, started the car, and followed them. "Especially if one of them is carrying a sledgehammer."

Gatlin laughed. "And you see how he rushed us up outta there when the coke hoes got there," he observed.

"Yeah, I know. Eliza is fine as hell."

Gatlin shook his head. "She's a crackhead!" he all but shouted.

"I know. All I'm saying is she's a fine-as-hell crackhead."

"And for a pocketful of rocks she can be all yours," Gatlin said sarcastically.

He stopped at the light and glanced over at Gatlin. "And her crackhead friends wasn't bad either."

"No, they weren't. One of them was kinda fine, for a crackhead. But they're crackheads!"

Becket gave Gatlin the finger. "Let's just go get this money."

"Right. I know you wanna rush back, see if you can't get in on that set."

"Look at that, caught in the act of being himself," Becket said because Gatlin was right. He was in a rush to get back to Winder's because Eliza was a fine-as-hell crackhead, and he was getting some of that. "Fuckin' right I wanna get in on that set."

"I know, 'cause Eliza is fine as hell."

"Glad you agree. Now call Andre and tell him to have the shit ready when we get there."

Gatlin called Andre, and he had the money ready when they got there, and he did the same with Butch. Now that they had completed their assigned task, Becket drove back to Winder's apartment. They rang the bell, and a shirtless Winder opened the door.

"That was quick."

"He was highly motivated," Gatlin said.

When he opened the door and let his men in, Eliza and her dick-sucking crackhead friends were naked, and Kalisha had the pipe in her mouth.

"This way," Winder said and led them into the bedroom.

"Here you go," Becket said and handed Winder the bag of money.

He opened the bag and looked in. "Any problems?"

"Butch talked his usual shit," Gatlin said.

"Okay." Winder handed them both some money. "Holla at me tomorrow." He left the room, and they followed him out. Gatlin started for the door, but not Becket.

"Is there enough here for me?" Becket asked, smiling at Eliza, who was smiling at him.

Winder laughed. "Y'all have y'all fill. I don't give a fuck."

"I'm good," Gatlin said as he continued slowly toward the door. "I told Cassidy I would take her to dinner tonight," he said, and after Chantelle sucked his dick, Gatlin left Winder's apartment and went to pick up Cassidy.

When he arrived at her apartment, he called out to her, but she didn't answer. When he went into the bedroom, he found Cassidy stretched out across the bed.

"You ain't ready?" he asked.

"Ready for what?"

"I told you I was gonna take you to dinner."

"You tell me a lot of shit that don't happen."

"Well, we're going out to dinner tonight, so get up and get ready."

"Okay, let me put some jeans on and do something with my hair and I'll be ready." Cassidy grabbed her Cinq à Sept jeans and put them on.

"Hurry up. I'm starving."

"Where we going?" she asked on the way to the bathroom to do her hair.

"To that Italian place on Park Street you like," Gatlin said and sat down on the bed.

"Primi Piatti?" she shouted from the bathroom.

"I guess that's the name of it."

Cassidy came out of the bathroom with the curling iron in her hair. "We're going to that Italian place on Park Street that I like so you can go to the comic book store."

"Yeah."

"Slick."

"What's slick about it?" he asked, and Cassidy didn't bother to answer.

When she was finished with her hair, Gatlin and Cassidy left their apartment and drove to Primi Piatti. They went to the comic book store first. Gatlin picked up a vintage copy of *Black Panther #4* from July 1977, which was in great condition, that the owner was holding for him. When Gatlin and Cassidy came out of the store, he was excited.

"In this issue, Black Panther is locked in a mystical battle with the Collectors! But first, Panther discovers Zanda's loyalties are with her kingdom. Is she a friend or foe?"

"I'm sure you'll find out," Cassidy said as they walked away from the store.

After dropping the vintage comic book off in the car, Gatlin and Cassidy made the short walk down the street to the restaurant. He reached for the door handle just as Martel walked up behind him and shot Gatlin in the back of the head.

Cassidy screamed as his blood hit her face, and she watched Gatlin's body fall to the ground.

Martel walked calmly down the street and dropped the gun in a garbage can. Then he walked back to his car, got in, and drove away.

Now they were even, and the peace could begin.

Chapter Twenty-two

For Alexis and Imani, it was building inspection night. They had already done the basic inspections: the framing, foundation, insulation, mechanical plumbing, electrical, and HVAC inspection had all been completed prior to purchase. Now that they owned the property, their plan was to evaluate the exterior and interior of the property: the roof, ventilation, wood, concrete drives and drainage, and walkways. The windows and doors, all electrical outlets, baths, banisters, outlets, stairs, and railings all needed to be evaluated. And then the pair of new hotel owners planned to go room by room that night to see what they had.

"This is just me throwing something out there, but I think we should throw everything out, gut it all, and start over," Alexis suggested. It was after ten, they had been at it since seven, and they still had two more floors to check.

Imani put her clipboard down on the table in the room and sat down. "I know. Option one is looking like the choice."

When they began the process, they saw several options, four to be exact. They could do option three: paint, get new carpeting throughout the property, and give the lobby and common areas a facelift. Option two included all of option three but called for new furniture and fixtures throughout the property. Or, as Alexis suggested, they could throw out all of the furniture, fixtures, and carpet, even knock out a few walls, and start over. That was option one.

"Make the name Plaza stand out and mean something," Alexis said.

Since the hotel was profitable, option four was to do nothing and let the property generate income for them. Since doing nothing wasn't an option, at least not for Alexis and Imani, they kept on checking the rooms.

"So, how's Brock?" Alexis asked.

"Brock is fine."

"I half expected him to be here, checking rooms with you."

Imani giggled. "And you know, under normal circumstances, he would be. He would have insisted."

"I sense a 'but' coming," Alexis said as they moved on to the next room.

"But he and my father are in Yemen."

"Yemen? What are they doing in Yemen?"

"Business."

"Business?"

"Taking our operation global." Imani opened the door to the next room. "They're there talking to people who are in contact with the Houthi movement."

"And I take it that those are the rebels."

"You would be correct."

"Global, huh? That's excellent, Imani," Alexis said, nodding her head. She was very competitive with Imani, and she was feeling a bit jealous for no reason at all. Imani's business was guns, hers was drugs, and there was no comparison between the two.

"Brock is a good man and a good man for business."

"Sounds like he is."

"So, what's going on with you?"

Alexis's face lit up as if she were saying, "What took you so long to ask?"

"Ronan is in town."

Imani slapped her hands together. "That's why you've been bouncing around all night, got your 'fuck me' pumps on," she said of the Aquazzura lace mesh stiletto pumps with the four-inch heel that Alexis had on. "Grinning like you got a secret."

"Guilty."

"How is he?"

"He's doing great. He's in town for a lawyer's conference on immigration law at the Ritz-Carlton in Amelia Island."

"How's he like Houston?"

"He said Houston is nice. He said that he's the token black man at the firm he works for." Alexis giggled. "He calls himself the spook who sat by the door. So, he's adjusting to that, but other than that, he said that he is very happy there."

Imani unlocked the door, and they went in to inspect the next room. "You know, I gotta say this."

"What?"

"You really fucked that up."

"I know."

"Ronan was a good man."

"I know he was."

"I mean a Brock Whitehall kinda good man," Imani said and went into the bathroom to check it.

"Imani!" Alexis all but shouted.

She stuck her head out of the bathroom. "What?"

"I know what a good man Ronan was, and I am well aware that I was the one who fucked it up."

"Oh. Sorry."

"It's okay." Alexis dropped her head and headed toward the door. "It's just that you're not the only one reminding me of what a good man Ronan was and how it was me who fucked things up between us."

"Ronan?"

Alexis nodded. "Even when he's not saying it. He doesn't have to. Just being with him is a reminder of how I pushed him away and eventually ran him to Houston."

"Is he married?"

"No," she said softly, and Imani saw the way that she floated around the room.

"You're still in love with him, aren't you?"

"Yes, I am," she said, admitting to Imani what she had yet to admit to herself.

"Why did you push him away?" Imani asked as they moved on.

Your brother came to Jacksonville.

Just as things between Ronan and Alexis were heating up, Hareem had moved to Jacksonville, and shortly thereafter, he brought the Miami Boys to town with him.

"I had a lot going on those days." Alexis giggled. "Did you know that he thought we were into each other?"

"No," Imani exclaimed with a shocked look on her face.

"Yes. He told me last night that he thought that the reason or one of the reasons we were having problems was that you and I were seeing each other and we just hadn't come out yet."

"You're kidding, right? Please tell me you're kidding."

"No, Imani, that is what he thought."

"I hope you straightened him out on that," Imani said definitely.

"I did. I told him that we were not gay," Alexis said firmly, even though each woman was a little bi-curious about the other, and neither would be opposed to an opportunity to explore it if one ever presented itself. "And I told him all about you being all in love with Brock."

"Good. I'm glad you cleared that up. I would have been so self-conscious around him if I saw him." Imani sat down at the table in the room. "You know what?"

"What?"

"The more I see of these rooms, the more I agree with you. Throw everything out, gut it all, and start over."

Alexis sat down at the table with her. "Option one is looking like the choice."

Imani leaned back and pointed at the walls around her. "Knock out all these walls, get an architect in here, and redesign the entire space. Make the name Plaza stand out and mean something."

"You are preaching to the choir. I am with you all the way."

"So, you ready to call it a night?"

"I think so. I'll put a call into my guy at Duval Engineering Group tomorrow."

"And I know somebody at Randolph Architects. I'll give her a call, too." Imani paused. "How much longer is Ronan going to be in town?"

"For the rest of the week."

"You know, if you wanted to spend some time with him, I could handle things here."

"I was thinking we shut down the top floor, throw out the furniture, knock down the walls, and go from there."

"Alexis."

"Yes?"

"I got this. Spend some time with Ronan."

"You sure?"

"Unless you don't want to."

"No, no. I want to. Thank you, Imani."

"You're welcome." Imani stood up. "And, Alexis?"

"Yes?"

"Try not to fuck it up this time."

Chapter Twenty-three

Now that they had settled on a course of action for their new property, Alexis and Imani said good night, and Alexis made the forty-five-minute drive to The Ritz-Carlton on Amelia Island. When Ronan opened the door and let her in, he kissed Alexis hungrily, as they stumbled into the wall. He pinned her against it, and then he kissed and sucked her neck and chest. Her fingers roamed wildly across his body. Alexis unbuttoned his shirt, rubbed his chest, and lathered his neck and chest with kisses.

They looked into each other's eyes. Ronan reached for her face and pulled her toward him. Their tongues became entangled in passion. He unzipped her dress, allowed it to fall to the floor, and then he took off his pants. He kissed Alexis again and gently laid her body down on the bed. He lay next to her.

It was just then that her phone began to ring.

Both Alexis and Ronan looked into each other's eyes and then at her purse.

She knew who was calling.

It couldn't be anybody but Cameron.

Alexis immediately flashed back to a situation just like this, only it was Hedrick calling. It was shortly after the Miami Boys had come to town. Hareem had just robbed two of their dealers, and she'd lost major product. Alexis was naked and wet, and Ronan was rock hard and moving toward her when her cell rang.

"I have to take this," Alexis had said that night and took the call. Once Hedrick told her what had happened, she told Hedrick, "I'm on my way."

That night, Alexis apologized to Ronan, told him the best lie she could come up with, got dressed, and left him in bed with a promise to return when her business was done. She did come back of course, and when she did, Alexis brought her A game and left him curled in the fetal position on his side of the bed, shaking and saying, "Don't touch me." But for Ronan, that night was the beginning of the end for them. One month later he was entertaining the offer from Cary, Estrada, Walsh & Associates.

Alexis could hear Imani's voice saying, *"Try not to fuck it up this time."*

She shook her head. Not this time.

Alexis gently pushed Ronan onto his back, straddled his body, grabbed his dick, and eased herself down on it. She rode him slowly while he feasted happily on her plump nipples. He began to feel her legs trembling on his thighs, and he pushed harder. Alexis bore down on him and increased her pace, pounding her hips furiously onto Ronan until she reached a very loud and violent climax.

In the morning, Alexis woke up feeling amazing. They made love, and then Alexis got up, and while Ronan got ready to attend his conference, she made the drive back to Jacksonville, singing.

I'm every woman
It's all in me
Anything you want done, baby
I'll do it naturally
Whoa, whoa, whoa

When she got home, Alexis showered and dressed in a Veronica Beard Kadar printed high-low dress and Stuart Weitzman Playa leather knot sandals and headed out for the day, still singing.

On the way into the office, Alexis stopped at Starbucks and got her usual grande cappuccino, but since she was in a very good mood that morning, Alexis ordered a double smoked bacon, cheddar, and egg sandwich and drove to the office thinking about her Diamond life.

It occurred to her now that Cameron and Martel agreed to stop the killing, maybe she could do as Imani suggested and spend some time with Ronan before he went back to Houston. She parked in her space, thinking that the night before was wonderful. The love they made was wonderful. Ronan was a wonderful man, one whose company she thoroughly enjoyed.

Why not relax and have some fun for a change?

Alexis went inside thinking that it was time for Cameron to really step into Hedrick's role and handle things without feeling that he needed to call her.

"Do what you think is best and let me know. If you fuck up, I'll tell you."

She had been having variations of that conversation since Hedrick was murdered, but to this point, Alexis had come running every time he called.

"That ends today," she said aloud and turned on her computer.

With that thought in mind, instead of reviewing her schedule for the day and responding to the emails that she received the day before, Alexis picked up the phone and called Ronan.

"Hello."

"Hey, sexy man."

"This most certainly is a surprise."

"I know that you're getting ready for your first session, but I wanted to know if you were free tonight."

Ronan paused, not to think about whether he had plans, but to be thankful because he had literally just prayed for this to happen. "No, my sweet, I have no plans for the evening."

Ronan wanted to be with her, even if they did nothing but have more incredible sex. He hadn't intended for it to happen. He thought that since he was going to be in town for the week, why not give Alexis a call? He figured they'd get together, he'd fuck her a couple of times, and he would head back to Houston.

What Ronan hadn't counted on was those old feelings resurfacing. He thought that he had taken those feelings that he had for Alexis, put them in a small box inside a box inside a black box, and stored them away deep in his mind, never to be thought of, much less experienced, ever again.

Compartmentalization is a beautiful thing.

"What did you have in mind?"

"I was thinking that I could come pick you up after your last session, and we could have dinner together, and then Dylan Lincoln is appearing at the Comedy Zone of Jacksonville."

"He's funny."

"As hell. So, you interested?"

"I am. Very interested."

"Great. What time does your last session end?"

"I could blow off the entire day if you want," Ronan said and paused to see if Alexis would bite on that. "But the last session ends at four."

"Okay, it's a date," Alexis said, and then she hedged her bet. "Now you didn't just meet me, so you know how crazy my day can get."

"Yes, my sweet, I am well aware."

"So, I will call you later to confirm. Sound good?"

"Sounds good. They're getting started, so I will look forward to your call."

"Have a good day."

"You too," Ronan said, and he ended the call and couldn't help but think, *here you go again.*

Alexis had cast her powerful spell over him, and he was powerless to resist her. So he was excited, even though he knew that he was setting himself up for possible disappointment. Ronan was excited about having dinner with Alexis.

And not to worry. When she blows you off for dinner, she'll make it up to you at bedtime because that's the Alexis Fox I know, he thought and went into his session.

It was early in the afternoon, and Alexis was showing a property.

"This house will steal your breath away as soon as you walk in. It has beautiful flooring and a spacious kitchen with plenty of counter and cabinet space. It has an open floor plan, a fireplace, a Florida room, and a large master suite with walk-in closets. It has an en-suite bath with a separate shower and tub and includes a water softener system and newly replaced central heat and air system," she had told her clients when her phone rang.

She took the phone from her purse, glancing at the display as she walked. Knowing that it was Cameron calling, Alexis sent the call to voicemail. It was only in that second that she remembered that he had called the night before and she had ignored him. When the clients went to look around the house on their own, she called him back.

"What's up?"

"Gatlin is dead."

"I'll get with you later," Alexis said, ended the call, and got back to the client.

As Alexis continued showing the property, she glanced at her watch. It was just after one o'clock. She would have plenty of time to deal with the murder of another of her men and still make it in time to keep her plans with Ronan.

Once she finished with the client, Alexis drove to her condo to change, and then she called Cameron to find out where he was.

"I'm at Austin's on Main."

"Stay there. I'm on my way to you."

"You want me to order you something?"

"No, I'm good. See you in a little while," she said, and she drove there thinking about how Diamond was starting to take more time and was, once again, beginning to creep into her real life. It caused her to question which life was real, or was it all now just her life?

Chapter Twenty-four

When Alexis arrived at Austin's and pulled into the parking lot, Cameron came out and got in the Jaguar with her.

"What happened?" Alexis asked the second he closed the door.

"I don't know."

"What you mean, you don't know?"

"I mean I've been trying to find out, but I haven't heard anything."

"How did you hear about it?"

"I got a call from Trent talking about Gatlin was dead, but he didn't know anything else about it."

"You talk to his woman?" Alexis snapped her fingers. "What's her name?"

"Cassidy."

"Anybody talk to her?"

"I haven't been able to find her either."

"Damn it!" Alexis glanced at the dashboard clock. It was a little after two, so she still had time to deal with this and still keep her word to Ronan. "You check with Maxi? Maybe he knows where to find her."

Cameron took out his phone and called Maxwell. He told Cameron that Cassidy was at his family's house, and he gave him the address.

"I'll follow you," Alexis said, and Cameron got out of her car.

When Alexis and Cameron arrived at Gatlin's family's house, there were a lot of people there. Cars were parked on the grass, and there were people standing outside. While Alexis waited in the car, Cameron found somebody he knew and sent them inside to get Cassidy. When she came out, Alexis got out of the car and walked over to where they were standing. Cassidy looked at Alexis, and since she had no idea that she was Diamond, she rolled her eyes and turned to Cameron.

"What's up, Cam?" Cassidy said, and then she started to cry.

"I'm sorry about Will." He hugged Cassidy. "He was a good man." Cassidy nodded her head and cried harder. "Can you tell me what happened?"

Cameron let Cassidy go, and she tried to pull it together enough to tell him what happened.

"We were going to dinner, and this guy walked up and shot Will in the head."

"Did you see who it was?"

"No, Cam." She shook her head. "It all happened so fast. It was like he came outta nowhere," Cassidy said, and then she melted back into Cameron's arms, crying.

"I'm sorry."

Cassidy punched Cameron in the chest. "You find who did this, and you kill them for me." She punched him again. "You promise me that."

"I will. I'll find them, I promise."

When Alexis nodded, Cameron separated himself from Cassidy. She walked back to the car thinking about the pain that Cassidy was in over the loss of her man. Although she was in no way responsible for him being murdered, Alexis knew that, in a way, he was dead because of her. Will Gatlin worked for her, and that was the reason he was dead.

But that's the game, she thought as she walked. It didn't make Alexis feel any better.

"I'm gonna let you get back to your family."

"You promised," Cassidy said as she stepped away.

Alexis got into Cameron's car and watched as he spoke to a few people before he got in the car.

"Who do you think did this?" she asked impatiently.

"My first guess would be Hareem and Martel."

"Call him," Alexis demanded. "Let him know that you want to meet."

Cameron looked at Alexis for a second or two before he took out his phone and made the call.

"What's up, Cam?" Martel answered.

"We need to meet."

"I'm at the Popeyes on Soutel."

"I'm on my way." Cameron ended the call and turned to Alexis. "He's at the Popeyes on Soutel."

"Let's go," she said and got comfortable in Cameron's truck.

When Cameron pulled into the parking lot at Popeyes on Soutel Drive, he backed into a space and then checked his gun before he went inside. Martel was seated at a table, eating the popcorn shrimp combo, red beans and rice, and a biscuit.

"What's up, Cam?" he asked and took a sip of his mango lemonade.

"What's up?" Cameron sat down.

"You wanted to talk?"

"You heard about Will Gatlin?"

"I heard about it. What's up?"

"What you know about him getting killed?"

Martel sat back with the most indignant look on his face. "You think we had something to do with that?"

Cameron pointed in his face. "Did you?"

"Hell no." Martel leaned forward. "You and me sat down at Netta's and put an end to all that shit. I gave you my word that shit was over and behind us. Now you sit there and ask me if we had Will Gatlin killed?" Martel sat back and relaxed a bit. "But I understand why you had to ask," he said because he wanted to appear reasonable and not like the man who had killed him.

"I don't give a fuck if you understand. And I never said you had anything to do with it. I just asked if you knew anything about it."

Martel held up his right hand. "I swear on my grandmother's grave that we ain't have shit to do with it." Martel had grown up in the system, so he never knew his mother or his grandmother, let alone been to their graves.

"And I don't know anything about it. The night it happened, I was right here. Matter of fact, your boy Winder came in while I was here and hollered at me."

Cameron sat looking at Martel. "I don't think you would do anything to break the peace we made." He stood up. "I just needed to look you in the eyes and ask if you heard anything."

"You know me, Cam. I'm a man of my word."

"I respect that. You hear anything, holla," Cameron said and walked out of Popeyes because, whether he believed Martel or not, he didn't have any choice except to accept it.

"What did he say?" Alexis asked.

"What we expected him to say."

"That he ain't have shit to do with it," Alexis said, mocking the way Martel talked. "Let's go."

"Where to?"

"Take me back to my car." Alexis paused. "You believe him?"

"I believe he didn't do it himself. No, I don't. But I think the nigga knows who did it because he gave the order."

"I think so too."

"What you wanna do?"

"What you wanna do?"

"I wouldn't mind killing one of theirs and saying we don't know shit about it."

"Make that happen," Alexis said and said nothing else until Cameron dropped her off at her car and she told him that she would get with him the next day. She got in her car and checked the time. It was a little after four. Alexis started the car and called Ronan.

"Hello, Alexis."

"Good afternoon, sir. We still on for tonight?"

"We sure are," Ronan answered enthusiastically.

"Great," a now bubbly Alexis said. "I'm going home to change, and then I'm coming to get you."

"I have a better idea."

"What's that?"

"Why don't I Uber into the city and save you the ride out here?"

Alexis paused to think for a second. "Do you still remember where I live?"

"I do."

"I'll try to be ready when you get here," Alexis said, and she ended the call smiling and drove home.

LaLa sat in his car and waited. When he got the call from Cameron, he knew exactly who he was going to kill. Then Cameron busted his bubble.

"Don't kill anybody high-profile. She don't wanna go to war. This just a little payback for Will."

"Okay, I won't kill Chub," LaLa said, but he was disappointed because he hated Chub and had been planning his demise for a while. But he was Diamond's loyal soldier, so he did what he was told and picked another target.

"There that muthafucka go," LaLa said and started the car.

He watched as his prey for the day walked to his car, got in, and rolled down the window. LaLa pulled out and rolled slowly down the street until he had pulled up alongside the car.

"What's up, Jamarcus?" LaLa asked as he raised his weapon, shot Jamarcus twice in the head, and drove away. He called Cameron. "One down."

"Appreciated," Cameron said, and he called Alexis.

After a quick shower, Alexis dressed in a red Cinq à Sept strapless cocktail dress and Christian Louboutin metallic leather ankle-strap sandals and was ready when Ronan rang the bell. When she opened the door, he took her in with his eyes.

"You look amazing," Ronan said as he stepped inside.

"Thank you." Alexis walked away from the door. "I'll just be a minute."

"No rush, unless there is. Do you have reservations?"

"We do, but we have plenty of time to make them," she said from the kitchen.

"You know, on the ride down here, I was nursing this fantasy of getting here and you not being ready and opening the door wearing something sexy. You know, a little satin camisole and panties, trimmed in lace kinda thing."

Alexis came out of the kitchen and walked into his waiting arms. "What happened next?"

He kissed her. "We decide to skip dinner and the comedy club and have mad sex on every piece of furniture in the house."

Alexis kissed him. "That all sounds great, except I'm hungry, so let's go." She broke their embrace and started for the door with Ronan following her.

"Uber Eats?" he offered.

"Let's go, Ronan."

After dining on Sicilian seafood stew and filet mignon at Taverna, Alexis and Ronan had a great time laughing at Dylan Lincoln at the Comedy Zone of Jacksonville. When the show was over, they got in the car, and Alexis drove north toward Amelia Island.

"I see you still don't like men spending the night at your house," Ronan said, thinking that Alexis would never change.

"It's not so much that."

"What is it then?"

"I don't want to have to get up in the morning to drive you out here for your conference and have to drive all the way back so I can go to work," she said, but she knew Ronan was right.

Alexis didn't like men spending the night at her house for a number of reasons, all of them relating to her life as Diamond. She might give voice to blaming Hareem and the Miami Boys for ruining the relationship with Ronan, but she knew that they were just a symptom of a larger disease. Her Diamond life had gotten in the way as it had and always would.

But this wasn't that. Ronan was only going to be in town for another couple of days, and Alexis planned to relax, have some fun, and enjoy him while he was there. They were going to Amelia Island to have sex, and she was driving home in the morning.

Ain't nobody said anything about catching feelings again.

Chapter Twenty-five

It was early Friday morning, and the sun sliced its way into the room. Alexis opened her eyes and felt relaxed and refreshed. It had been a couple of days since Cameron had a second meeting with Martel. He assured them that there was peace between their two houses, and it seemed to be holding even after LaLa hit Jamarcus. She hadn't gotten a call from Cameron in a couple of days, so Alexis had been able to spend uninterrupted time with Ronan, and it had been good.

He spread her legs and got on top of her. "Good morning," Ronan said and entered her slowly and gently.

"Good morning," Alexis said and wrapped her arms and legs around him.

He attacked her tongue the way she liked it while he pushed himself deeper inside her. Alexis kissed and sucked his neck and rocked her hips, and he felt her juices drenching his shaft. The more he felt her body pounding against him, the harder he pushed into her with everything he had. She made slow circles around his nipples, and they got harder. Alexis spread her legs wider, and he continued to ease himself in and out of her.

"Cum hard for me," she demanded. "I want to feel you explode inside me."

Ronan held her tighter, and he matched Alexis stroke for stroke until he felt himself begin to expand inside her, moving in and out of her faster and harder until they both exploded, and they collapsed in each other's arms.

"That was so good," Alexis said after a while.

"And it keeps getting better."

She patted his leg. "That's what practice does for you,"
Alexis said and started to get out of bed.

Ronan grabbed her arm. "What's your rush?" he asked
and pulled her to his chest.

"I have a property to show at ten." Alexis pressed her
body against his and kissed him.

"You ever wanna be spontaneous and just up and go
somewhere?" He kissed her.

"Sometimes. But you know I'm more of a planning,
plotter kind of girl."

Ronan kissed her tenderly. "Let's do something spontaneous today."

"You have been trying to blow off that conference since
you got here," Alexis said, and their lips met again.

"That's because it is so majorly boring. I would much
rather spend the day with you."

"Not today. I have two properties to show today, one
this morning and another this afternoon, but after that,
I'm wide open. What were you thinking about doing?"

"Let's go to the islands for the weekend."

Alexis said nothing. She wanted to go, but in the ten
years that she'd been running her business, she had
never left the country. And was this the best time for her
to be out of the country? Sure, the peace had held for two
days, but there was no telling how long it would last.

"I know, I know, that is much too spontaneous for you,"
Ronan said, and Alexis could hear that the excitement
had gone from his voice.

"You're right, that is much too spontaneous for me."
Alexis held the back of his head and pulled his lips to hers.
She kissed him long and tenderly. "And that is exactly
why I'm gonna do it."

"Really?"

"Really. Where do you want to go?"

Ronan looked at Alexis and paused to think, not only about where he wanted them to go, but how he was really digging this new Alexis. "Turks and Caicos."

"I've never been to the Turks and Caicos before." Alexis and Bells used to travel all the time, and they were frequent Caribbean visitors. "Sounds good."

"You're serious?"

"Yes, Ronan. I am very serious. I wanna go."

"I'll make all the arrangements."

"No, buddy. No, you won't."

"What?"

"The last time I let you make the arrangements, you booked us into the bedbug hotel."

"Vegas." He kissed her and thought fondly about that weekend. "I would have married you that weekend—if you had said yes."

"I gotta go," Alexis said and kissed him one more time before she got out of bed and headed for the shower.

"Don't wanna talk about that, huh?"

"No, I don't wanna talk about Vegas." Alexis closed the bathroom door, thinking that maybe she should have accepted his proposal, told him the truth about who and what she really was, and changed her life.

Once she had showered and dressed, Alexis left Ronan to the last day of his conference, and she went home. While she was at the office, Alexis arranged for them to fly from Jacksonville International Airport later that evening to Miami.

After a two-hour layover, they departed and flew to Providenciales International Airport in Turks and Caicos. When they arrived on the island, they were taken by limousine to the Seven Stars Resort and Spa, where Alexis had reserved a one-bedroom oceanfront suite.

That night, they made love on the balcony with the moonlit sky in the background. He reached for her shoulders, grabbed her hips, and entered her. Alexis was so wet and he was so hard that he began to pump it in her as hard as he could. The feeling of her spasming pussy around him felt so amazing. She bucked as he pounded her from behind. When she felt his body jerk, she used her muscles to tighten around him.

They slept late that morning and ordered room service before noon. They ate on the balcony where they had made love hours before. Over breakfast, the subject of what they were going to do for the day came up.

"So, Mr. Spontaneity, what do you wanna do today?" Alexis asked.

"Ms. Plotting-planner didn't plan our entire day?"

"No. I just got us here and got us a place to sleep."

"Okay. How about this." Ronan wiped his mouth and put the napkin down. "I say we have sex, and then go to the beach. After that, we do whatever comes our way."

"I like that plan," Alexis said, and they went inside to make love.

The world-famous Grace Bay Beach was a gem of the Turks and Caicos islands. Its white sand beaches were absolutely breathtaking with water a perfect shade of aqua, and there were few rocks or seaweed to speak of. While spending some time on the beach, they met a couple that came to the island every year on vacation. They said that they were going snorkeling at the Bight Reef. Since it was a day of spontaneity and neither Ronan nor Alexis had ever been snorkeling or had even considered it before, they accepted the invitation to join.

"Let's go to the outer buoys," the man recommended.

"We'll see a ton of different fish," the woman said, because they had been there before and gone snorkeling at the reef many times.

After that experience, which they enjoyed and promised to do again someday, Alexis and Ronan returned
to the hotel, where the concierge told them about a
two-hour champagne sunset cruise from Grace Bay that
was leaving from the hotel in an hour.

"What do you think?" Ronan asked. "You wanna sip a
glass of champagne and watch the sun set?"

"I wanted to go horseback riding on the beach, but I'm
down for the cruise if you are," Alexis said, and an hour
later, they set sail along the coastline of Grace Bay.

After the champagne cruise, they ate at Coco Bistro
and had Caicos lobster bisque and the Caicos lobster and
avocado spring rolls, which were made with Thai mango
and red cabbage slaw. They ended the evening dancing
the night away at Lucid Illumination.

As she walked barefoot along the beach, holding hands
with Ronan, Alexis thought about the wonderful day
that she had just spent. She squeezed his hand a little
tighter because she knew that tomorrow evening all this
would be over and it would be back to her double life on
Monday morning. But did it have to be like that?

Alexis had money, lots of it. She owned property, and
that part of her business was growing. She and Imani had
plans to buy more property, so the question that she
had to ask herself was, did she really need to keep living
her double life selling drugs, or was it time to put that life
behind her?

She looked over at Ronan. The entire time that he'd
been there, he'd been hinting at her about coming
to Houston. Not just to visit, but to live there. And
what would be so bad about that? Alexis had no ties to
Jacksonville. There was nothing to keep her there.

Now Alexis had to ask herself why she was still doing
it. Why was she living the double life of a successful real

estate agent and a ruthless drug queen pin when it could be standing in the way of what had the potential to be something wonderful?

This could be her future. This could be her life.

All she had to do was walk away and leave the drug life behind her.

Chapter Twenty-six

Since she didn't get a chance to do it the day before, Alexis woke up talking about going horseback riding. After having a room-service breakfast in bed, the couple went to the hotel spa, because as Alexis said, "What's the point of staying someplace with 'spa' in the name and you don't go to the spa?"

"I can't argue with your logic."

With that singular thought in mind, Alexis and Ronan spent the morning getting deep muscle massages to restore comfort, suppleness, and movement with blended aromatherapy oils to alleviate deep-seated tension in the neck, shoulders, and back.

When the afternoon rolled around, Alexis got to do what she had been thinking about doing since she saw the Provo Ponies sign. Neither Alexis nor Ronan had ever ridden a horse before, so they were assigned to the beginner's category and assigned a guide. They chose a private ride and headed out for the ninety-minute ride on the beautiful beach and in the waters of Long Bay.

As the afternoon turned into evening, Alexis and Ronan enjoyed a delicious meal of twelve-ounce center-cut New York strip loin and tuna loin at the Coyaba Restaurant before sadly returning to the Seven Stars Resort and Spa to pack so the limousine could take them to Providenciales International Airport for his flight to Houston and her flight to Jacksonville.

Since his flight was leaving first, they were waiting at his gate. When Alexis made the reservations for them, she asked if he wanted to change his original return flight to Houston and fly out of Turks and Caicos.

At the time, it made perfect sense. "Why fly back to Jacksonville only to catch another flight to Houston the following morning?"

It didn't make sense, therefore, he told Alexis, to book his return flight out of Turks and Caicos, and now he wished he hadn't. Now, as the minutes ticked away, he wanted to spend every second of each of those minutes with Alexis, and she wanted to spend that time with him. She was considering changing her flight and flying to Houston with him. Alexis could just as easily catch an early flight in the morning and be in the office in the afternoon. Or she could take the day off to check on both her legitimate and illegitimate business. It had been almost a week since she'd spoken to Cameron.

Ronan took her hands in his. "What are you thinking about?" he asked.

"You and me—walking on the beach last night," Alexis lied since she couldn't tell him what she was really thinking. A life without Diamond would be a life where she didn't have to lie to him all the time.

"That was nice."

"It was."

"There are no beaches in Houston, but Galveston is an hour's drive away."

"It's something that we should do again," Alexis said and rested her head on his shoulder.

"I had a great time with you this week, and I don't want it to end."

"I enjoyed being with you too."

"Then come back to Houston with me." Ronan paused to summon his courage. "I love you, Alexis. I've been in love with you since the day we met, and my running away to Houston and the passage of time hasn't done anything to change that love. I know now that I never want to spend another day without you."

"I love you too, Ronan," Alexis said. Even though she wasn't trying to catch feelings, she did love him. At one time, she loved him very deeply. "And I will think about it. But I have a lot going on in my world right now, so I can't, even if I wanted to, just up and move to Houston."

"I understand. You just bought a hotel in Jacksonville, so I get it," Ronan chuckled. "Your world is complicated."

"What's so funny?"

"You told me that your world was complicated when we met, and I arrogantly said that I was up to the challenge and could deal with whatever you had going on." Ronan chuckled. "Then I wimped out and ran away to Houston."

"You sure did." Alexis paused to summon her courage. "When you left, it broke my heart. I understood why you made that decision, but it broke my heart. What made it worse is knowing that it was me that pushed you away."

"I am so sorry. I love you, and I never wanted to hurt you." He brought her hands to his lips and kissed them tenderly. "Let's correct our mistake. Let's try again."

"I'd like that. But please, you have to be patient with me."

"I've waited all this time without you, wasted time, I think, so I know that I can be patient and wait for the best thing that ever happened to me."

Alexis kissed him on the cheek. "That is so sweet of you to say."

"I meant every word."

"I know you did." Alexis paused. "I've never been to Texas."

"I would be more than happy to show you the great state of Texas. All you have to do is visit."

"I am gonna come see you. I promise," Alexis said, and Ronan began to shake his head.

"Not good enough. Let's set a date for you to visit. You know, Ms. Plotting-planner, a plan."

"Two weeks," Alexis said quickly. "But you do understand that is subject to change."

"Of course. I mean, you are Alexis Fox. I don't expect you to change overnight. But if you can be patient with me, and I could be patient with you, I am sure that you and I can have something amazing and rare."

"I can do that," Alexis said, and the lovers suddenly got sad.

"Good evening and welcome. Southwest Airlines flight service to Houston, Texas, will begin boarding shortly."

Ronan stood up. "I guess that's our cue," he said downheartedly and held his hand out for Alexis.

"I guess it is."

Ronan took Alexis in his arms. "I hate saying goodbye."

"So do I."

"So, I'll just say I'll see you in two weeks. Give you a big sloppy but romantic kiss, and then go get in line."

"Goodbye, Ronan. I'll see you in two weeks," Alexis said.

And after a long, passionate kiss, Ronan got in line, and a somewhat melancholy Alexis started for her gate, thinking that this life could be hers and all she had to do was give up her Diamond life. The question that Alexis had to answer was, was she ready to do that?

Chapter Twenty-seven

Since her good friend Imani owned a limousine service, a car was waiting for Alexis when she returned to Jacksonville. Although she didn't tell them that she was going, as the driver drove away from the airport, Alexis thought about calling Cameron and Maxwell to let them know that she was back and have them come to her condo to find out what had been going on while she was on the islands. It didn't take long to talk herself out of that one.

Alexis had thought about and replayed her conversation with Ronan over and over during her flight back to Jacksonville. She was getting comfortable with the idea and was seriously thinking about putting her drug life behind her, so there was no way that she was going to rush back to it.

"Whatever they got going on will keep until tomorrow," she said aloud.

Therefore, Alexis went home, took a long bath, and went to bed missing Ronan.

The following morning, Alexis got back into her routine. She dressed in a Kobi Halperin floral peasant dress and Christian Louboutin patent leather pumps, and then she stopped at Starbucks for a spinach, feta, and egg white wrap and a grande cappuccino, and then it was off to the office. It was late in the afternoon when she called Cameron and Maxwell and told them to meet her at the condo at nine o'clock.

"Come on in," she said when they arrived.

"What up, Diamond?" Maxwell asked.

"How's it going, Diamond?" Cameron asked as they walked into the condo.

"Help yourselves to drinks if you want."

"You want something?" Maxwell asked as both men went to the bar.

"I'm good." Alexis sat down in her Queen Anne chair. "I haven't heard from you two this weekend. What's been going on?"

"Everything has been quiet for a change. We've gotten back to doing business as usual."

"Nobody dead? No problems with Hareem and Martel?"

"Nope. I haven't heard anything from them niggas, and ain't nobody died."

"That's good to hear. What about you, Maxi? Everything good in your world?"

"Shit yeah, I've got no problems." Maxwell chuckled. "Muthafuckin' Winder getting on my nerves, and I been thinking about killing him, but other than that nigga, everything is all good."

"What's up with that? What's he getting on your nerves about?"

"Because he's a whiny bitch, Diamond," Maxwell said.

"He really is," Cameron concurred. "The nigga ain't ever satisfied with shit. He always got a complaint about something, or somebody ain't treating him right."

"Pitiful." Alexis shook her head. "And this is the man you brought me to replace Hedrick?"

"He kept pushing for a meet with you—" Cameron began, but Maxwell cut him off.

"You mean the nigga kept whining like a little bitch about a meeting with you," he corrected. "'Why won't Diamond sit down with me?'" Maxwell said, imitating Winder.

"Yeah. But he's a good earner, and he runs a good program, so even though I knew what you were gonna say, I let you come to your own conclusions."

"Smart," Alexis said and thought that maybe with time he could be able to replace Hedrick. However, this was the first time she had heard about Maxwell having problems dealing with Winder.

At that same time, in another part of the city, a similar conversation was taking place.

"That muthafuckin' nigga Maxwell about to make me catch a case!" Winder shouted after he hung up the phone.

"What he do now?" LaLa asked.

"This nigga done played me off again. He and Cam both know that I want to sit down with Diamond, but he keeps telling me I need to talk to him. Shit! If he could do what I needed him to do, I wouldn't need to sit down with Diamond."

"You know Diamond talks to who she wants to talk to," Jarell said.

"Shit, she barely talks to me, and I've been with her for years," LaLa added.

"Fuck that, LaLa! At least the bitch does talk to you. She sees me, the bitch rolls her eyes and goes the other way."

"Maybe you got bad breath," LaLa laughed. "I don't know."

"Fuck you, LaLa. I'm tired of all them niggas disrespecting me. And I ain't gonna take the shit much longer."

"What you gonna do about it?" Jarell asked.

"Thinking about making a move."

"What kind of move?" Jarell asked.

"I've been thinking about switching sides," Winder said, and he looked carefully at Jarell and LaLa to gauge their reactions. He couldn't read LaLa's stone face, but Jarell's eyes lit up.

"Hareem?" Jarell questioned.

Winder nodded. "I've been talking to Martel."

"And?" Jarell asked.

"And what?" Winder asked.

He was still looking at LaLa and thinking maybe he shouldn't have said anything in front of him, but he had heard him complain about Cameron and thought he'd be more receptive.

"And I'm gonna talk to him again."

"You know it was probably Martel who killed Ross and Gatlin, right?" Jarell pointed out.

LaLa laughed. "Probably? Everybody knows it was that nigga."

"That's my point. Diamond can't protect us from them niggas because she's scared of them." Winder chuckled. "Can't beat 'em, join 'em."

"So, you going with Hareem and them?" Jarell asked.

"For better product."

"Shit. For a better product, I'd be interested in making a move," Jarell said.

"What about you, LaLa?"

"For better product, I'd be interested in hearing what he's talking about," LaLa may have said, but he wasn't the least bit interested. Diamond did speak to him, she always treated him with respect, and he had no problem with her. LaLa also believed that honor and loyalty were important and actually meant something. He looked at the disloyal muthafuckas in front of him and was disgusted by them.

"I'm going to meet Martel today. Why don't the two of you ride with me and you can hear for yourselves what he's talking about?"

"Bet," Jarell said excitedly.

"That's cool," LaLa said because it never hurt to listen.

An hour later, the three men arrived at Sweet Mama's. When Winder got out of the car, he saw that Martel was there, but he wasn't alone. He was sitting in the window, eating, and Chub was with him.

Winder looked at Jarell and LaLa. "He's not alone."

"What that mean?" LaLa asked.

"Nothing." Winder paused. "I didn't know he would be here, that's all. One of you needs to wait out here."

LaLa shook his head. "You go ahead."

"You sure, LaLa?" Jarell said.

"Yeah, you go ahead, and you can tell me what the nigga's talking about." He leaned close and whispered, "I'll watch your back. I don't trust Martel."

"I hear you."

"I got a bad feeling about this," LaLa said.

"Why?" Winder wanted to know.

"I told you. Because Martel killed Ross and Gatlin."

"That shit is behind us," Winder insisted.

"I know. Cam sat down with them and settled that shit. But I still don't trust him."

"Cam ain't settle shit." Winder tapped his chest. "It was me and Martel who made this peace."

"Whatever way it went, them the niggas who killed Hedrick, Ross, and Gatlin, and I don't trust them," LaLa said.

"Then what you doing here?" Jarell asked, and Winder wanted to know as well.

"This is business. Trust the nigga or not, I'm interested in better quality product so I can make more money. So, you go ahead and let me know what the nigga talking about."

"Cool," Jarell said and followed Winder into a crowded Sweet Mama's.

Martel and Chub were in a booth in the back by the window, eating—meatloaf with collard greens and mac and cheese for Martel, and Chub was tearing up some pan-seared pork chops—when Martel saw Winder come in with Jarell. He waved them over to the table.

"What's up?" Martel asked.

"Sup?"

"This my nigga, Chub," Martel said, and Chub barely looked up from his food. "You Jarell, right?" Martel asked, but he didn't appreciate Winder bringing Jarell with him. Martel thought that if Winder got on board, he would handle his own people.

"Right."

"So, what's up?" Martel asked.

"I'm ready to make that move," Winder said.

"Good to hear, good to hear," he said, and Chub nodded. "I'm going to assume that since you're here, you're in too."

"Slow down, big boy. I came to hear what you talking about."

Martel cut his eyes at Winder. "I'm gonna tell you like I told your boy here. What you gonna get is premium pricing on a superior product."

"We'll talk more about that later," Winder told Jarell.

"But you in, right?" Martel asked.

Winder nodded his head quickly. "I'm in."

"Cool, cool. From now on, you talk to Chub," Martel announced, and Chub wiped his mouth and stood up.

"Come on, let's talk," he said and went to sit down at another table, and Winder followed him.

Jarell stood for a second or two looking at Martel before he nodded his head in respect and left Sweet Mama's.

"What's the nigga talking about?" LaLa asked when Jarell walked back to the car, shaking his head.

"He said what you gonna get is premium pricing on a superior product."

"That's it?"

"Yeah. That's it."

"No details."

He pointed toward Sweet Mama's. "I guess that's what him and Chub are talking about now."

LaLa shook his head. "I got a bad feeling about this."

"Me too, LaLa, me too."

Chapter Twenty-eight

It was late in the evening when Martel turned off Palm Forest Place onto the long driveway and drove past the circle with the water fountain that was surrounded by palm trees and parked in front of the house that he admired so much. He got out of the car.

"How are you doing, Miss Kimberly?"

"I'm fine, Martel. Come on in."

"Thank you."

"Hareem and the baby are out by the pool."

"He ain't got that baby in the water, do he?" Martel asked as he followed Kimberly through the house.

"No. Some say different, but that baby is too young for the water. They're just sitting out there," she said as they got to the door.

"Thank you, Ms. Kimberly," Martel said, and he went outside to the pool.

"Marty-mar!" Hareem shouted when he saw him coming.

As Martel got closer, Omeika started to cry at the sight of him.

So much for her getting used to him.

Hareem got up and got his daughter out of the stroller and picked her up.

"What's up?"

"My crying-ass daughter," Hareem said and tried to quiet her.

"Why you always got her? Where's her mama?"

"She had an appointment somewhere," he said as Martel sat down in one of the lounge chairs by the pool. Hareem sat down in the chair next to him with a now quiet Omeika in his arms. "She called and said she'll be back soon, and then I'm outta here."

"That don't answer my question." Martel put his feet up. "Why you always got her?"

"You don't get it, Mar. This is where I wanna be. You know what it's like growing up without a father. That's not gonna happen to her."

Martel nodded solemnly because he understood. "You know I get it."

"I knew you would."

"What's up with you and Loonie?" Martel asked because he knew how Hareem felt about her.

"Unfortunately, nothing. Loonie ain't got no interest in me being anything other than a good father to our daughter."

"Then what's she doing living in your house?"

"Pop got her living here. That way he gets to see Omeika all the time." Hareem reached over and got her bottle. "So, what's up?" he asked and gave Omeika her bottle.

"I wanted to tell you that you were right."

"I'm right about a lot of shit."

"You were right about recruiting Diamond's people instead of killing them."

"I told you. Who you got?"

"Winder and Jarell came to see me at Mama's. Winder is definitely in, and I'm pretty sure Jarell will come along. LaLa was there, but he didn't come inside, so I don't know about him."

"I don't know them other two, but Winder, that's big." Hareem stood up and put Omeika back in her stroller. "That's gonna hurt her."

"I know. That's why I recruited him. That was Hedrick's boy."

"He might be able to bring Hedrick's whole team with him." Hareem nodded. "Keep doing what you're doing. I don't think you need to kill anybody else, but you keep doing what you're doing. Eventually, Diamond will be gone," Hareem said, thinking that Imani and his father had been right all along. This was how he would have it all.

He glanced at Martel, and that was when he noticed the look on Martel's face.

"What?"

"What you mean, I don't need to kill anybody else?"

"Ross. And that other nigga . . ." Hareem tapped the arm of the chair. "Gatlin. As soon as I heard about them getting killed, and getting killed the way they did, I said to myself, that ain't nobody but Marty-mar." Hareem laughed.

"You know me too well," Martel said, laughing.

"Especially when I heard that Omar was in town but not Griff." He nodded and smiled at Martel.

"You right."

"Of course I am."

"Don't go getting the big head."

"My sources tell me that there was another body at Ross's apartment that lost a lot of blood that the cops didn't find. Griff?"

Martel nodded. "Dead."

"Rest in peace," Hareem said. "I never liked that nigga, but rest in peace."

"He was my cousin, but I didn't like the nigga either."

"Yeah, I knew that shit. But now I'm thinking that you doing what you do is why we're able to recruit her people now."

"We always made a good team," Martel said and fist-bumped Hareem.

"Since the day we met."

"So what's next?"

"I told you. You keep doing what you're doing. Diamond don't wanna fight us. Hedrick was her power, and Cameron can't handle it."

"Naw, that nigga soft." Martel stood up. "I'm out."

Hareem stood up. "Where you off to?"

"Make some money, watch some hoes, get some pussy, you know, my usual," Martel said and started to go inside the house.

"Get with me tomorrow," Hareem said, walking along-side him and pushing Omeika's stroller into the great room.

"What you got up?"

"Nothing major. I want you to come down to the port with me. There are some people I need to see."

"Who?"

"Reed Allen and Miller Ford."

"Who are they?"

"Port inspectors," Hareem said, and Martel smiled and nodded.

It would be the first time since Imani gave Hareem control of the shipping ports in Jacksonville that he asked Martel to come with him. He understood how important the port was to Hareem and to their business, so he was happy to be getting involved in that part of their business.

"I'll get with you tomorrow," Martel said and opened the front door. Imani was standing there looking in her purse for her keys.

"Hey, Martel," Imani said and walked by him. "Hey, Hareem."

"Hey, Imani," Martel said and watched Imani walk inside the house. "How you doing?"

"I'm fine, Martel. How are you doing?"

"You know me. I'm always gonna be all right."

"That's good," Imani said, taking Omeika's stroller from Hareem, and she turned toward the great room.

"Like I said, I'm out."

"Get with me around eleven," Hareem said as he walked out with Martel.

"See you tomorrow," Martel said, and Hareem went back inside.

When he went back into the great room, Imani had put Omeika back in her playpen and was sitting on the couch playing peekaboo with her.

"What's up with Martel? He come to tell you who and how many he killed today?"

"You're funny."

"When I wanna be, but I'm serious. Who'd he kill to-day?" Imani had heard on the news about the rash of drug-related murders and knew that Martel was respon-sible.

"Nobody." *At least not today.* "He came to tell me that instead of killing Diamond's people, he's been recruiting them."

"How's that going?"

"He said it's going good."

"Your idea?" Imani chuckled. "Had to be."

"Yeah, it was my idea. I told Marty-mar not to kill them, recruit them. That's how you take over her business without firing a shot."

"What did he say to that?"

"You know Marty-mar." Hareem chuckled. "He said it was much easier to just kill them all. But I convinced him that going to war is bad for business."

"Excuse me?" Imani questioned, not being able to believe her ears.

"You heard me. I convinced him that going to war is bad for business."

"Wow. Going to war is bad for business," Imani said slowly, nodding her head as if it were a novel concept. "I wonder where you got that idea from."

"Stop it, Imani." Hareem smiled at his sister.

"No, seriously, where did you ever get an idea like that?"

"You wanna hear me say it, don't you?"

"Oh, I do. I really do," Imani said with a satisfied and superior look spreading across her face.

"I got it from you, and you were right. So was Pop."

"He's been through it, and he saw how his penchant for violence destroyed his business. And it left him weak when he needed to go to war. We've been trying to share that wisdom with you, but you just didn't seem to get it."

"Couple of things changed that."

"Getting shot being one. What's the other?"

"Something Pop said to me."

"What was that?"

"He said when he was young, he thought he had to prove something to his father, and that was why he did a lot of shit, trying to prove he was smarter and better than his father. It made me realize that I was doing the same shit. Trying to prove to both of you that I knew what I was doing."

"And you didn't."

"I know that now, Imani."

"Well, you didn't. We'd try to tell you something, and you'd go do the exact opposite."

"True. But I'm listening now—to every word he got to say." Hareem shook his head. "Ain't no better consigliere than Pop. Been there, done that, taught a course on it. That's Pop."

Imani patted Hareem on the leg. "About time you realize that and take advantage of that wisdom and experience. The game hasn't changed since he played it. The only difference is now it's us playing the game."

It was then that Kimberly came into the great room. "Dinner is ready. Loonie isn't back yet, is she?"

"No, ma'am."

"You wanna wait for her?" Kimberly asked, and Imani looked at Hareem.

"No. I'm gonna eat and get outta here," Hareem said, getting Omeika from her playpen.

Imani breathed a sigh of relief. "Good, because I was starving and I didn't feel like waiting."

"You watch Omeika until she gets home?" Hareem asked as they made it into the dining room and sat down at the table. Their father was already seated at the table and waiting for them.

"No problem. I got little miss."

"Thank you," Hareem said as Kimberly came into the dining room carrying a serving pan.

"What's for dinner?" Imani asked.

That night Kimberly had prepared cauliflower-broccoli salad, chicken parmesan, saffron rice, roasted brussels sprouts, and garlic bread. After they blessed the food, they helped themselves.

"I want you to know that I am proud of you," Imani said once she had filled her plate.

"Why?" Hareem questioned with a mouthful of chicken parm. "What I do?"

"You're evolving. I never thought I'd say this, but you really are evolving, and I want you to know that I'm proud of you, and so is Daddy."

"I can speak for myself. But I'm proud of you too, boy," Mr. O said and started eating.

"Thank you." He chuckled. "I never thought I'd hear y'all say it."

Just then, they all heard the front door close.

"Where is everybody?" Loonie shouted.

"In here!" Imani shouted back.

Loonie came into the dining room and saw the food on the table.

"So, y'all wasn't gonna wait for me?" Loonie got a plate and sat down.

"No," Imani said without looking up and kept eating.

Chapter Twenty-nine

It was ten thirty when Alexis pulled into her garage and turned off the car. It had been a long day. She had shown a couple of properties and had a couple of closings, so it was a good day, but when she left the offices of South Jacksonville Realty, her day wasn't over. After stopping off to grab a gyro combo to go at the Gyro King, Alexis drove to the Plaza Hotel and Suites. Seeing that nobody on site was expecting her, the front desk staff was caught off guard when one of the new owners walked in carrying a to-go bag from Gyro King.

After eating her gyro and fries in the manager's office, Alexis walked the property. Throughout the day she had been thinking about their plans for the hotel. Once the decision had been made to eventually throw out all the furniture and fixtures, knock down the walls, and start over, she and Imani had decided to keep the hotel open and close one or two floors at a time until the renovations were complete. Alexis had made an appointment to speak with an architect at Duval Engineering Group about designing a new room layout.

However, as she thought about the plan throughout the day, Alexis began to think that maybe they should go in a different direction. She had come to the hotel that night to explore the feasibility. After walking the property, she returned to the office and began reviewing the occupancy, personnel records, and maintenance reports. When she was finished with that, Alexis crunched the numbers and then called it a night.

As soon as she came through the door, Alexis tossed her keys in the dish and kicked off her Manolo Blahnik pumps. She went to the bar, poured a glass of wine, made herself comfortable on the couch, and called Imani.

"Hey, Alexis," Imani answered.

"Hey, Imani. This isn't too late, is it?"

"No. I'm still in my office at the house, going over the room occupancy report, daily forecast report, and F and B report."

"Looking for anything in particular?"

"Not really, but kinda. You know me, always thinking."

"Well, I just got home from the hotel."

"You should have called me. I would have met you there."

"Now that I'm talking to you, I should have, but I was up there, like you, reviewing reports, and I was thinking—"

"Which is always dangerous." Imani giggled, and Alexis ignored the comment.

"That maybe we should consider going in a different direction."

"I'm all ears."

"I was thinking, dangerously as you say, that instead of closing a floor or two at a time, we close the hotel and begin renovations. It will reduce the time and make more of an impact when we reopen the all-new luxury Plaza Hotel and Suites."

"You're right, it would make more of an impact, especially if we work the local press right. But what about the employees?"

"They currently work for REJ Management for another week. At that point, REJ is going to stop paying them. So, unless we technically hire them by assuming responsibility for funding payroll like we originally planned, they are unemployed." Alexis took a sip of wine. "We were going to reevaluate the staff anyway. My plan is to give them all eight weeks' severance pay, which I think is more than fair."

"I think that's too much, but go on."

"We let them know that some people will get hired by the new company, and some won't. That will give us time to reevaluate the current staff, decide which ones we want to hire, and begin hiring for the other positions and have them trained and in place when we reopen." Alexis paused. "What do you think?"

"I think that the blanket eight-week severance is generous. Most severance packages arc something like two weeks for every year the employee worked. But other than that, and we can work that out—"

"I know we can."

"I like the idea. We would definitely make a much bigger splash closing and reopening in a much grander style. I like it."

"I knew you would."

Now that she had Imani on board with her new plan, Alexis took off the Elie Tahari Mia striped midi-dress that she wore that day, took a long, hot bath, and went to bed.

She woke up early that next morning thinking about Ronan. She had an eight o'clock meeting that morning with the architect at Duval Engineering Group. Once she was dressed and out the door, Alexis called Ronan on the way to her meeting. Since Houston is in a different time zone, it was just after six when Ronan's phone rang, so she woke him up.

"Hello."

"I woke up thinking about you," Alexis said softly.

"I wake up every morning thinking about you. That's probably because I go to sleep every night wishing you were here."

"I wanna see you."

"I always wanna see you." He yawned and stretched. "So I guess I'll see you this weekend? I hope, I hope, I hope."

"I have a meeting this morning at eight that I'm on my way to now. But after the meeting, I was thinking about flying to Houston. Catching an early flight back in the morning."

"I will rearrange my schedule."

"Great. I'll call you back when I make flight arrangements."

While Alexis was waiting for her meeting at Duval Engineering Group to begin, she made reservations on a nonstop flight that was leaving Jacksonville at eleven fifty-five and arriving in Houston at one thirty-four.

It was perfect, and Ronan was there waiting when she arrived. Once their lips parted, they walked hand in hand to collect her luggage and began their time together.

"I didn't know how you wanted to spend the time we have together, so I planned for everything."

"Did you now?" Alexis rested her head on his shoulder as they walked.

"I did. I didn't know if you wanted to spend a romantic evening exploring the Houston nightlife."

"That sounds nice."

"If that's what you want to do, I have the entire evening planned. Now, if you wanted to spend what little time we have together locked in each other's arms, making passionate love until your flight leaves in the morning, I have that covered as well," he said when they arrived at the carousel.

"And that would be?"

"I have a suite reserved at the Marriott."

"Is there a third option?"

"Of course. We go back to my house, order takeout, and watch a movie. You choose," Ronan said as her luggage arrived.

"I wanna do it all. I wanna spend a romantic evening with you, and then I want you to make me scream and shake until my flight leaves in the morning."

"Done." Since his plans for their romantic evening began with dinner, Ronan raised one finger. "To the Marriott!"

As soon as they arrived in the suite he had reserved, Ronan made Alexis scream and shake until it was time to go to dinner at an elegant restaurant called Beauchamp's that boasted of its sophistication and ambiance.

After dinner, and as the sun was setting, Ronan arranged to take Alexis on a sightseeing helicopter tour of the Houston skyline. The thirty-minute ride flew over the Galleria and downtown areas.

"That was amazing!" Alexis exclaimed once they were back on the ground. "I've never done anything like that. And it was so romantic with the sun setting in the background."

"I'm glad that you liked it, but I'm not done."

"Are you trying to impress me?"

"Yes, Alexis, I am definitely trying my best to impress you. And might I add that that was a stupid question." He smiled as they got back to his car.

"Granted." She giggled. "What else do you have planned for our evening?"

Ronan made a sweeping gesture toward the car. "Your chariot awaits."

They left there and closed out their evening together at the Rooftop Cinema Club, snuggled up, eating popcorn and watching a romantic comedy in an Adirondack-style love seat.

"Did you enjoy your evening?" Ronan asked as they were on their way back to the Marriott.

"I did. Very much." Alexis leaned over and kissed Ronan on the cheek as he drove. "Thank you for arranging all of this for me."

"You're welcome."

"What about you? Did you enjoy yourself tonight?"

"I did. But I always have a good time with you."

"You do. But that's only because I'm so much fun to be with." Alexis laughed, and so did Ronan.

"And you're so modest. That's what I like best about you."

"And all this time I thought you were only interested in my body." She smiled.

"I like that too. But it's that big brain of yours that really does it for me."

"Glad to know I'm more than just a pretty face to you."

"So much more. You're a drop-dead gorgeous face to me."

Alexis took a playful swing at him.

"It's dangerous to beat up the driver while he's driving."

She hit him on the arm. "I'll keep that in mind for next time," Alexis said, and then there was quiet in the car as Ronan thought about how he was going to ask his question. He nodded his head and inhaled deeply.

"I don't want you to think that I'm pressuring you or anything, but I wanted to know if you thought any more about moving here."

"No, you're not pressuring me, Ronan." She reached for his hand. "And, yes, I have thought about it."

"And what do you think?"

"I think that I am not totally opposed to it." She squeezed his hand. "I mean, things are looking like they might stabilize in my business. Once that happens, I promise that I will seriously explore the possibilities."

"I love you, Alexis. You know that, and I want us to be together." Ronan laughed. "I think I've made that plain. I want to spend the rest of my life with you," he said, and Alexis got quiet because he really didn't know her. In a sense, he was in love with a lie. The lie that she allowed her closest friends to believe.

She glanced over at Ronan and thought about telling him the truth about who she really was. Alexis thought that he deserved to know, and then he could choose if she was truly the woman he wanted to spend the rest of his life with.

Ronan chuckled. "Let me shut up before I scare you off."

Alexis said nothing for a second or two. "I have something that I need to tell you. Something I've needed to tell you for a long time."

"This sounds serious. What did you want to tell me?"

Alexis inhaled and summoned her courage. "I'm not the woman you think I am."

"Okay, who are you?"

"Truth is . . ." Alexis paused. "I'm scared," she said, losing her nerve just that quickly.

"What are you scared of?"

"I don't know," Alexis lied.

She knew exactly what she was scared of. Alexis was scared that if Ronan found out the truth about who she really was, he wouldn't love her anymore. Ronan deserved a choice not to be in love with a lie.

"That one day you'll wake up and realize that I am not the woman you think I am. It's why I've always kept you at arm's distance and why I ran you away from me."

"Then don't do it. Don't push me away this time."

"I wish it were that easy," Alexis said and knew that it could be easy. She could give up her Diamond life and allow him to truly get to know her.

"It is that easy—or at least it is for me. I know what I want. I just don't know if you do."

"I do know what I want," Alexis said definitely. "I've known for a long time what I want, and I have put my mind, my body, my heart, and my soul into getting it. So, please, be patient with me while I expand that carefully crafted vision to include you."

"I can do that. Tell you what."

"What?"

"Next time you come on the weekend, let's spend some time driving around greater Houston, not the tourist stuff."

She smiled. "You mean the stuff we've been doing?"

"Yes, that stuff."

"But I have enjoyed every minute of it."

"Well, you should have. I went out of my way to make sure that you did. I want you to come back again and again, and again." Ronan may have chuckled, but he was serious about what he was saying to her. "I want to show you where you're going to be making your money—selling houses and investing."

"That's a good idea. It will help me in my decision process."

"Or I could move back to Jacksonville."

"No," Alexis said quickly and firmly. "I think I'm ready for a new experience," she said instead of telling him that she wanted him nowhere near Jacksonville and her Diamond life.

"I completely understand," Ronan said as he arrived at the Marriott, and he parked his car. "So." He turned the car off and glanced at Alexis. "You wanna fuck?"

"Yes."

Chapter Thirty

It had been two weeks since Alexis returned from her second trip to Houston, and she was enjoying the peace. She hadn't spoken to Cameron in two days, and that had given her the opportunity to focus on the renovation of the Plaza Hotel. During that time, she had gotten with Imani, and they met with architects from both Randolph Architects and Duval Engineering Group. After sharing their vision and looking over preliminary designs, they decided to go with Marguerite Spears of Randolph Architects.

The project had moved forward to the schematic design phase of the project. Now that they had discussed the project and any requirements, Marguerite was doing an analysis of the property, zoning, and building code issues that may affect the specific development. Now she and Imani were considering acquiring Southwark Plaza. It was a fully leased retail center with an anchor grocery store. The fact that the property would give them the ability to increase rents to market rates over time made it seem like a sound investment that would diversify their portfolio.

"South Jacksonville Realty, my name is Alexis Fox. How can I help you today?"

"Good morning, Ms. Fox."

"Hey, you," she said when she heard Ronan's deep voice. "How are you doing today?"

"I'm great. Calling to make sure we were still on for this weekend."

"We sure are."

"Great. And I wanted to know if there was anything or anyplace in particular that you wanted to see or do while you're here."

"No, not especially. This weekend is all about you, my dear," Alexis said as her other line began to ring. "As much as I'd love to spend the day swooning over your sexy voice, I have work to do."

"So do I, but I am never too busy to talk to you. Talk to you later," Ronan said quickly before Alexis could comment.

"Bye," she said and took the call. "South Jacksonville Realty, my name is Alexis Fox. How can I help you today?"

"My name is Jana Izolda. I was referred to you by Eino Alfson, and I'm interested in buying a house, and I'd like to move on it pretty quickly."

It was like that all day. The phones were ringing off the hook, and since she had no properties to show that day, Alexis spent the day in the office, fielding calls and making appointments. By the end of the day when she left the office, Alexis was tired and ready to go home, but she thought it best to check in with Cameron to see what had been going on in her house.

As she drove away, the implication of her not hearing from her people for days at a time wasn't lost on her. It meant that Cameron could handle it as Hedrick had before him and maybe she didn't have to be as hands-on as she had been. That would leave her free to explore other opportunities, and that included a life and a future with Ronan.

"What's up, Diamond?" Cameron answered when she called.

"What's up, Cam? Meet me at the condo."

"I'll be there in about an hour," he said, and Alexis ended the call.

When Cameron arrived at the condo, he told her that everything was cool except Maxwell hadn't heard anything from Winder in a couple of days and he owed him a chunk of money.

"You need to get on top of that."

Meanwhile, in another part of Jacksonville, Maxwell was trying to resolve the situation with Winder. He had spoken to Winder, and he said that he had the money. Arrangements were made, and Henderson was sent to the place where Winder said he was going to be to collect the money he owed. However, things didn't go the way that he planned.

"He didn't show," Henderson said when he called.

"This muthafucka gonna make me kill his ass. He keep fuckin' with me," Maxwell said.

"What you want me to do?"

Maxwell paused to think. "Give him another half hour. If he doesn't show by then, come on back here."

"Cool, a half hour," Henderson said, and he ended the call.

"What's up?" D'shaun asked when Maxwell tossed his phone on the coffee table.

"This nigga Winder been bullshittin' me for days about my money."

"What's up with that?"

"I don't know, but he gonna fuck around and be out of business, he keep fuckin' with me," he said as the doorbell rang and he went to answer it. "What's up, LaLa?"

"Making this money," LaLa said as he always did. "What's up with you?"

"This muthafucka Winder owes me twenty large, and now the nigga is fuckin' ducking me."

"You don't know?" LaLa asked.

"Don't know what?"

"That you probably ain't gonna hear nothing from Winder."

"Why not?"

"Because he's with Hareem and them now."

"What the fuck you say?"

"I said that Winder is working for Hareem now."

"That muthafucka!" Maxwell said angrily. "How you know?" he demanded to know.

"Because I was there when he met Martel and made his move. Jarell jumped ship too."

"When was you gonna tell me that shit?"

"I didn't think I had to. I thought the nigga would be man enough to tell you himself," LaLa said and sat down.

"Fuck is you sitting down for? Let's go get that nigga," Maxwell said and went to arm himself. "You too, D'shaun."

When they got to the house where Winder did business, D'shaun kicked in the door and opened fire. Maxwell and LaLa came in behind him firing. Winder, Truevon, and Becket were caught totally off guard. Winder fired two shots as he moved toward the back of the house. Truevon shot at D'shaun and hit him with two shots to the chest.

As Maxwell approached, Truevon got up from the couch and pulled the trigger, but his gun was empty. When he turned to get away, he fell to the ground. As he scrambled to his feet, Maxwell kept walking and raised his weapon. He took aim and shot Truevon in the chest, and he went down from the impact. Maxwell stood over him and kicked Truevon in the face and then shot him in the chest.

Maxwell saw that Winder had run into one of the bedrooms. He centered himself and kicked in the door. He stepped into the room quickly and saw Winder standing by the window. Winder shot at Maxwell, went out the window, and ran. Maxwell rushed to the window and fired a couple of shots at Winder, but he was gone. He went out after him.

When Winder heard Maxwell coming behind him, he turned and fired a couple of shots. Maxwell fired back and kept coming. He stopped, aimed, and shot Winder in the back of his head as he ran back into the house. The impact took him off his feet, and he landed on his face. Maxwell came into the house and stood over Winder's body. He shot him twice in the back.

"Muthafucka," he said and shot him again.

Maxwell felt the pain in his stomach. That was when he realized that Winder had hit him with his last two shots. Maxwell dropped to his knees.

"Shit," he said just before he fell over and died next to Winder.

LaLa had been exchanging shots with Becket, but when he saw Maxwell go down, he knew that it was time for him to get outta there. He fired a couple of shots at Becket and made a run for the door. Becket fired a few shots that bounced off the doorframe.

"Fuck!" Becket shouted and went after LaLa.

He came out of the house running, and before long, he saw LaLa running to get to a car. When he heard him coming, LaLa turned and fired a couple of shots and moved to take cover behind a car. As Becket approached the cars, he stumbled, and the gun went off. The shot hit LaLa in the stomach. He shot back and shot Becket in the chest, and he went down from the impact.

As LaLa walked up to him, Becket pulled the trigger, but his gun was empty. Becket tried to get to his feet, but he fell back to the ground. He stood over him and kicked Becket in the face. Then LaLa put one in his head.

Chapter Thirty-one

The River City Marketplace was an outdoor shopping mall on the north side of Jacksonville, and most nights it was where you could find Cameron. The reason that you could find him there was because Dawnesha James worked as a bartender at Chili's Grill & Bar. Like Alexis, Cameron was enjoying the peace and had gone to the movies and had sex with Viera Stone earlier that evening, and now it was time to close out his evening with Dawnesha. He would go by there, have a couple of drinks, get something to eat, and when the restaurant closed, he would go home with Dawnesha.

"Hey, Cam," she cooed and leaned on the bar when he sat down. "How you doing?"

"I'm good, I'm good. What's crackin' with you tonight?"

"Ready to get outta here." Dawnesha picked up a menu and handed it to Cameron. "You want something to drink?"

He opened the menu. "Surprise me."

Dawnesha smiled because there was a drink she'd been dying to try and a particular mood she wanted Cameron in when she got off work and got him back to her place.

"You got it."

While Dawnesha made his surprise drink, Cameron looked over the menu. He hadn't eaten anything since he choked down a steak, egg, and cheese biscuit for breakfast. *That and fuckin' Viera always makes me hungry for some reason,* he thought.

When Dawnesha returned, she placed a drink in front of him.

"What's this?" he asked, smiling at the orange-colored drink that was made with cherry brandy, dark rum, golden rum, white rum, 151-proof rum, four different juices, and a dash of grenadine.

"Try it first and I'll tell you," Dawnesha said and pushed the glass closer to him.

Cameron took the straw to his lips and took a sip. "That's good. It's strong, but it's good. What is it?"

"It's a Zombie," Dawnesha said proudly.

"Yeah." Cameron nodded. "I like that." He chuckled and took another sip. "This might be my drink from now on."

"I'm glad you like it. Do you want something to eat?"

"Yeah, I'm starving." He opened the menu again. "Gimme the Ultimate Smokehouse Combo."

"I'll put that in for you," Dawnesha said, walking away, and Cameron enjoyed the sight of her hips swaying from side to side.

Baby got ass for days, Cameron thought, shaking his head.

It was just about that time when LaLa turned into the River City Marketplace and made his way around to Chili's. He saw Cameron's Toyota Tundra backed into a space. He parked next to him and turned off the car.

"I knew he'd be here," LaLa said, taking out his phone to call Cameron again. He'd been calling since he left the shootout at Winder's house, but Cameron hadn't answered. Knowing that Cameron was a creature of habit, LaLa knew to come there.

"Why ain't he answering?"

LaLa took a deep breath and moved the cloth away from his wound. He had taken a shot to the stomach when Becket stumbled and the gun went off.

"Just bad luck," he said, thinking that he never should have gone with Maxwell to try to get his money back. He should have known it wasn't gonna be a polite conversation, but he wasn't expecting him to tell D'shaun to kick in the door either.

Wasn't no conversation to be had at that point.

He pressed the cloth harder against the wound and opened the car door. LaLa had to steady himself before he started walking toward the building. When he stepped inside, he saw Dawnesha behind the bar, pouring drinks. He tried to get her attention, but she looked away.

"Damn."

LaLa saw Cameron at the bar and went that way.

He saw LaLa coming. *Fuck is this nigga doing here?* Cameron questioned. "Sup, LaLa?" he asked when he got closer.

"We need to talk outside," LaLa said. His knees got a little weak, and Cameron had to catch him.

"Fuck wrong with you? You fucked up or something?" Cameron asked, and that was when he saw the bloody cloth pressed against LaLa's stomach. "Oh, shit. Come on."

As quickly as possible, Cameron got LaLa out of there and took him to his truck. Once he had him inside, Cameron got in, started up the truck, and drove away fast. As soon as his phone connected to the Bluetooth, he called Alexis.

When the call came through, Alexis was relaxing in the tub with a glass of Rombauer chardonnay. "What's up, Cam?"

"I need you to call Jelena Grey and tell her I'm coming."

When Alexis heard the name Jelena Grey, who was a physician's assistant, she knew without having to be told that somebody had been shot. "Damn it! Who is it?"

"LaLa."

"I'll make the call and meet you there," Alexis said, and she ended the call.

Cameron looked over at LaLa as he drove. His eyes were closed. Cameron tapped him on the shoulder a couple of times. "Hey, hey, LaLa."

He jumped and opened his eyes.

"Don't you fuckin' die on me. Who did this to you?"

"Winder."

"Winder? Winder shot you? Why?"

"No." He shook his head and coughed. "Becket shot me." He coughed. "Winder flipped."

"Flipped? What you mean Winder flipped?"

"Winder owed Maxwell money, so me, Maxwell, and D'shaun went to get his money. Him and Jarell work for Martel now. They're dead."

"Who's dead?"

"Everybody." He coughed. "Maxwell, D'shaun, Winder, Truevon, and Becket, all dead," LaLa said and coughed.

"Hold on, nigga. We almost there. You make it, you gonna get all this blood out my truck," Cameron said, and LaLa laughed a little. "Bleeding all over my fuckin' truck."

When Cameron got to Jelena Grey's house, she had the porch light on and was standing in the window. She rushed out when she saw the truck pull into her driveway.

"Get him inside." Cameron carried LaLa inside. "Put him on the table," she ordered, pointing to the dining room table as she grabbed her bag.

Once she stopped the bleeding, Jelena cleaned the wound. She was getting ready to find and remove the bullet when the doorbell rang.

"That's probably Alexis." She kept working on LaLa. "Go let her in, please," Jelena said and quickly realized that she had referred to Alexis by her real name instead of Diamond.

Alexis? Cameron asked himself as he went to answer the door. *That must be her real name.*

"How's LaLa?" Alexis asked as soon as he opened the door.

"She's working on him now," Cameron said and led Alexis into the dining room.

He'd always assumed that Diamond was her real name. After all, Diamond was the name Bells introduced her as on the first day that he met her, and he never thought to ask.

Alexis and Cameron stood quietly as Jelena worked on LaLa. Once she had found the bullet and removed it, she removed the pieces of shattered bone that had come from his rib cage, and then Jelena closed and dressed the wound.

"Is he gonna be all right?" Alexis asked when she finished.

"He'll be fine," Jelena said and gave her instructions for aftercare.

"Thank you, Jelena," Alexis said. "I'll take care of you tomorrow."

"No rush . . . Diamond," Jelena said deliberately, careful not to call her Alexis again.

She had met Alexis when they were both students at Florida International University. Alexis was working on her master of science in finance degree, and Jelena was working on her master of health science degree. Years later, when Hedrick was shot, Alexis, knowing that she couldn't take him to a hospital, called Jelena. She came right away and saved Hedrick's life. From then on, anytime Alexis had a problem like that, she knew that she could depend on Jelena.

"I know you're good for it, Diamond."

Jelena went back to the dining room to be with her patient, and Alexis went into the living room with Cameron and sat down.

"Did LaLa tell you what happened?" Alexis asked.

"He said that Maxwell's dead."

"What?" an already shaken Alexis asked.

"Maxwell, Winder, D'shaun, Truevon, and Becket. He said they're all dead."

"How? What happened?"

"Maxwell told you that Winder owed him money, right?"

"Right," Alexis said impatiently, wanting Cameron to tell her what happened.

"LaLa said that him, Maxwell, and D'shaun went over there to collect. I'm guessing there was a shootout. I don't know. Somehow LaLa got away and came to me." Cameron paused. "One more thing,"

"What's that?"

"LaLa said that Winder had started working for Martel. Jarell too."

"Damn it, Cam!" Alexis shouted. "How y'all let that shit happen?"

Cameron said nothing. Maxwell was supposed to be keeping Winder in check, but he knew Alexis wouldn't want to hear that. He was running things for her, so it was his responsibility to make sure that everybody stayed in line.

"Go check it out," Alexis said angrily. "Go by Winder's house and check it out. Then you find out what's going on with Jarell. I wanna know if it's true. I wanna know if he betrayed me. And I wanna know who else."

"I'm out," Cameron said and headed for the door. He would ask if Alexis was her real name another time.

"Come by the condo when you got something to tell me," Alexis barked as he opened the door and left.

When Cameron got to Winder's house, every light seemed to be on. Based on what LaLa said about the shootout, he expected to get there and find an active crime scene, but there were no cops or ambulances there. He got out of the car, took out his gun, and approached the building. The front door was open, so he stepped inside. Maxwell's and Winder's bodies on the floor by the door with the guns still in their hands was the first thing he saw.

"Damn, Max."

Cameron lowered his gun and continued to walk through the house. Eventually, he came upon D'shaun's and Truevon's bodies. He looked around to see if he saw Becket's body anywhere, but he didn't.

Once he had collected their stash, Cameron was about to leave when he thought that once the cops found this scene, they would be all over them. He went into the kitchen and pulled the stove away from the wall. Cameron pulled the gas line and then started a fire in the house. He got out of there just before the house exploded in flames. Cameron watched it burn for a while before he left there.

His next stop was Zabumba's, a club where he knew Jarell liked to hang out. He went inside and looked around. When he saw him at the bar, Cameron took out his gun and walked toward him.

Jarell saw him coming, and not knowing what happened earlier that night and thinking that he and Cameron were cool, he would tell him what was up with Martel. It was just business, and Cameron, being a businessman and not a hothead like Maxwell, would understand. He smiled and raised a glass.

"Cam!" he shouted.

"You with Martel and them now?"

"Yeah, I was gonna talk to you about that," Jarell said and was reaching for his gun.

"Nothing to talk about. Nobody betrays Diamond," Cameron said and shot him in the head.

Cameron left Zabumba's as quickly as possible. He got back in his truck and drove away from Zabumba's and headed for Alexis's condo to report what he had found.

Chapter Thirty-two

It had been over a week since Maxwell's death, and Alexis was in mourning. In one night, she had lost five of her best people, and LaLa was still recovering from the wounds he sustained that night. Sure, some good people stepped up and gladly filled those spots so the beat didn't stop and the money kept flowing, but that hadn't made the losses any easier for Alexis to take.

She tried to rationalize it by telling herself that Maxwell's death wasn't that deep, he was just a man who sold drugs for her, but she knew in her heart that nothing could be further from the truth. Maxwell had been an integral part of her business and her life since the day she met him, Hedrick, and Cameron. Hedrick may have been her workhorse, the man she counted on to get things done for her, but Alexis felt a special kinship with the man she called Maxi. Anytime Alexis needed to make a point and be brutal about it, Maxwell was always at her side.

With everything that was going on in her world, Alexis had given serious consideration to getting out of the business and moving to Houston with Ronan. She had to question why she was still doing it. Alexis had established her own legitimate property business as well as her expanding partnership with Imani. The truth of the matter was that Alexis Fox had money, and if she chose to be honest with herself, there was no reason whatsoever for her to still be doing it.

When Bells was murdered and she stepped in, it was out of her love for him and it was a challenge to her, and Alexis never backed away from a challenge. Could she successfully run a criminal organization and maintain her real life as a real estate agent? She did it and had been doing it well for years until now.

Now, the cost of doing business, which now included the lives she'd lost, was getting expensive, and Alexis had to ask herself if she wanted to keep paying the price. When it all began ten years ago, she was a different person and it all seemed worthwhile, and then there was the money. When Bells was murdered and she took over his business, Alexis realized how much money he was making and how much he had hidden from her. It was more money than she could, at the time, imagine. Living the double life of a successful real estate agent and a drug queen pin was exciting to her, but now it had lost its luster.

"What are you going to do today?" Ronan asked.

"I have an appointment to meet the contractor at the Plaza. But that's it."

She had taken a few days off from the real estate office to clear her head, make some decisions about her future, and focus on building her legitimate business. During that time, Ronan had been very encouraging and supportive. All he knew was that Alexis had lost a friend and he needed to be there for her. He wanted to catch the first flight to Jacksonville so he could go to her close friend's funeral, but Alexis knew that she could not allow that, mostly because she didn't go.

As badly as she wanted to go and pay her respects to her fallen soldiers, she knew that it would be a bad idea. There was no telling who would be there, and with the chance that somebody would recognize her as real estate agent Alexis Fox and realize that she and Diamond were one and the same, the risk was way too high.

"How's the demolition going?"

"Fine. They should have the entire building gutted by next week."

"Have you and Imani settled on the design of the rooms yet?"

"Not yet, but I think that we are close on the lobby and common area designs."

"How is Imani?"

"She's great. I am so lucky to have people in my life like you and Imani. If it weren't for the two of you, I think I would have lost my mind." The problem with that was, as supportive as Ronan and Imani had been, she couldn't be honest with either of them, so nobody really understood what she was going through.

"That's good," Ronan said. "I hate to go, but I have a meeting with a client who needs an estate plan."

"You have fun with that, and I'll talk to you soon."

"I love you."

"I love you too," Alexis said, and then she hung up the phone.

And that was the other thing that was complicating her world. She had, once again, fallen in love with Ronan, so the idea of giving up the life and starting a new life with Ronan was starting to have a haunting pull on her.

Alexis glanced at her watch. She needed to be at the Plaza in two hours to meet the contractor, and she needed to get moving. She forced herself out of bed and ran a hot bath for herself. Feeling relaxed, refreshed, and renewed after a good soak, Alexis settled on a Valentino Manifesto silk bandana top, silk-twill Manifesto bandana-print wide-leg pants, and Valentino Garavani leather clogs, grabbed her hard hat, and headed out for the day.

When Alexis arrived on site, the contractor was late, so she walked the property and saw that things were progressing as planned. The men working had ripped out the entire interior down to the studs.

"Looks different from the last time you saw it."

"It really does," Alexis said to her general contractor, Anthony Tortora. "How are you doing today, Anthony?"

"Fair to partly cloudy. How are you today?"

"I'm awesome."

"Well," Anthony said and started walking with Alexis walking alongside him, "let's see if you still feel that way."

"Oh, no. What's wrong?"

"I discovered some unforeseen damage that may cost much more to repair than budgeted."

"Like what?"

"We found quite a bit of rotted framing."

"Show me," Alexis said, and he led her to one of the spots he'd identified.

"We also found the presence of asbestos. Not that much," Anthony said quickly, "but it is there, and we have to deal with it."

"What else did you find?"

"There are some damaged wires and pipes throughout the property. There's some minor decay damage, but that was to be expected."

"Right, we talked about this."

"We did." Anthony started walking. "Fortunately, there are no foundation issues that you'll need to deal with."

"That's something."

"It's something major, or it would have been if there were foundation issues. We didn't find any wrong place-ment of wires or pipes, and we didn't identify any missing essentials like pipes or beams."

"So, correct me if I'm wrong, but what I hear you saying is that other than the rotted framing and the presence of asbestos, we're not in bad shape here. Is that what I hear you saying?"

"That is what I'm saying."

Alexis relaxed a little. "When can I expect to receive your revised estimate?"

Anthony reached into his jacket pocket and handed Alexis an envelope as his phone rang. "I need to take this, Alexis. Look that over, and we'll talk later tomorrow," he said, walking away from her.

Since the lighting in the gutted building wasn't the greatest, Alexis went outside to read the revised estimate. "Shit!" she said and took out her phone.

"Hey, Alexis. What's up?"

"We have a problem."

"What's that?"

"I'm at the Plaza meeting with Anthony, and he said that we have quite a bit of rotted framing, and he found the presence of asbestos."

"Not good. What else?"

"There are some damaged wires and pipes throughout the property, and there's some minor decay damage."

"Is that it?"

"Isn't that enough?"

"Yeah, it's more than enough. But he did warn us to expect to have some of these problems."

"Yes, he did, and he wasn't kidding."

"I sense a 'but' coming."

"A big one."

"Tell me," Imani said and prepared to hear the worst.

"He handed me the revised estimate."

"Do I even want to hear how much?"

"No."

"Then don't tell me. What are you getting ready to do?"

"I'm going home."

"I'll come over there this evening and look it over," Imani promised.

"See you then."

After walking through the building again to look at the items that Anthony pointed out, Alexis went home to wait for Imani to get there. When she got there, she

poured herself a glass of cognac, because the new estimate called for something stronger than wine, and she
straightened up the living room. Alexis hadn't felt much
like going out, and cooking seemed like such a task, so
she'd been wearing out the Grubhub app and eating in
the living room while she binge-watched *Black Lightning*
on television.

Once she had removed all the trash from the coffee table, Alexis saw the phone that she used for her Diamond
persona. She had turned it off the day of Maxwell's funeral and hadn't turned it back on. Alexis started to turn
it on to at least check her messages. She was sure that
in the days it had been off, Cameron, more likely than
not, had left several messages. Alexis sat there on the
couch for a while, looking at the phone, and then she got
up. She took the phone to her bedroom and put it in the
nightstand drawer. She sat down on the bed and thought
about what putting the phone in the drawer meant.

Am I done? she asked herself as her phone rang.

"Hey, Imani. What's up?"

"Brock just got back from Yemen and—"

"And you can't stand to be away from him for another
second."

"Yes. So, is it all right if he comes with me?"

"Not a problem."

"Good. Open your door." Imani giggled. "We're outside."

"Coming," Alexis said and went to open the door.

"Hey. Sorry about the last-minute notice," Imani said
when Alexis opened the door, and she came in with Brock.

"Not a problem," Alexis repeated. "How are you, Brock?"

"I'm fine. Glad to be back," he said and kissed Imani on
the cheek.

"How was Yemen?"

"Hot. But productive."

"That's what matters, right?" Alexis said as they went into her living room. Imani and Brock sat on the loveseat. "Can I get y'all something to drink?"

"That depends." Imani glanced at Alexis's glass. "What are you drinking?"

"I'm drinking cognac."

"If you're drinking cognac instead of wine, then I'm drinking cognac too."

"What about you, Brock?"

"Cognac is fine, thank you."

"Three shots of Rémy VSOP coming up," Alexis said and went to the bar in her living room. While she poured their drinks, Imani and Brock whispered to each other about what was going to happen when they got to her condo. Alexis returned, and once she had handed them their drinks, she sat down on the couch.

Imani took a sip of her drink and then pointed at the file on the coffee table. "Is that it?"

"Yup," Alexis said, reaching for the file.

Imani got up and sat next to Alexis on the couch, and she handed her the revised estimate.

While Imani stared at the paper, Brock sat quietly and sipped his drink. His business was weapons, so he always tuned out when Imani and Alexis talked about real estate and construction.

"Wow," Imani said.

"I know."

"I mean, it's not that bad, but wow."

"It's not like we can't handle it, but wow," Alexis concurred.

"It's going to cut into some of the other things we were talking about moving on."

"Southwark Plaza?"

"Yes."

"What about St. Johns Square?"

"I think we can still do that. What was the asking?" Imani wanted to know.

"Let me get my laptop," Alexis said and got up to get her laptop from the office.

Brock watched her walk. "How's the ankle?" he asked.

"What?" Alexis asked, and then she remembered. "Oh, it's fine," she said and sat down with Imani, wondering what prompted Brock to ask about her ankle. When the shooting broke out at Hareem's birthday party and Mr. O got shot, she twisted her ankle when she tried to run.

"Running in four-inch peep-toe pumps is not a good idea, trust me," she remembered telling the paramedics while they treated her.

But that was months ago, so why would he just be asking about it now?

Brock didn't say much after that. He just observed Alexis. Since the night that he tortured and killed Hedrick, he'd been wondering how Diamond knew Mr. O had been shot, unless she heard it from somebody who was there at the party.

Alexis was there that night. She sprained her ankle, Brock thought.

He looked at Alexis and thought about the description he had gotten when he asked people who had actually seen her and could say what Diamond looked like and how she carried herself.

"Tall for a woman, honey brown skin, and beautiful," was what each said.

Everything else was about the Jaguar she drove, the designer clothes that she wore with sunglasses, even at night, and the amount of jewelry that Diamond always wore. Brock took a long, hard look at Alexis. She was tall for a woman, at least five nine or ten if he had to guess.

Her rich skin was honey brown, and Alexis most certainly was beautiful.

Imani glanced at Brock. "What are you over there thinking about?"

"The condo," he lied, but he was thinking that Alexis could be Diamond.

Chapter Thirty-three

Even though she wasn't going to South Jacksonville Realty, the morning ritual hadn't changed much for Alexis. She still got up around the same time, and after she laid out her outfit for the day, she showered, got dressed, and headed for Starbucks for her usual grande cappuccino. The difference was that those days, instead of going to South Jacksonville Realty wearing designer dresses and pumps, Alexis dressed in jeans, women's Timberland boots, and a hard hat, and her destination was the Plaza Hotel and Suites.

When she arrived, Imani was already there. Since she had her family's legitimate business, Luxury Private Charters, to run, she wasn't usually at the Plaza first thing in the morning, but she would come there at some point in the day, and Imani was there with Alexis every night. Imani was there that morning because they had a plan that they were working on.

After crunching the numbers of the revised estimate, Alexis and Imani decided that they would hold off on the Southwark Plaza project. However, they did not want to push back the St. Johns Square project, nor the one-hundred-unit apartment complex in Hollywood, Florida, that they planned to convert to condominiums, which they were looking to make an offer on. Therefore, Imani came up with a plan to get Anthony to offer them a discount on the revised estimate.

"Morning," Alexis sang when she came into the trailer that they had rented to work from.

"Morning, Alexis," Imani said and pointed to the cup-holder that Alexis was carrying. "I hope one of those is for me."

"It is." Alexis took a cup from the holder. "I got you a venti Caramel Ribbon Crunch Frappuccino." She handed it to Imani.

"Thank you."

Alexis dug in the Starbucks bag. "And I got you a spinach, feta, and egg white wrap."

"Thank you, Alexis. I left the condo this morning before Kimberly was out of bed, much less cooked breakfast."

"Must be nice having a cook."

"She's not a cook. She's part of the family. But it is nice to have somebody cook for us. Her cooking gives us a chance to eat as a family. It's something my father believes in."

"You don't cook?" Alexis asked and took a bite of her wrap.

"I can cook. I used to cook all the time, and I was a pretty good cook, too. But when we moved here and Daddy hired Kimberly and she cooked that first meal for us, that was the day I stopped cooking. I will tell anybody who will listen that the woman is incredible."

"Like I said, must be nice. I can cook. I just don't like to and really don't have the time."

"Since you don't like to cook, you should think about bringing somebody in to cook for you."

Alexis shook her head. "My schedule is too crazy."

"True, but your schedule is changing." Imani sipped her Frappuccino. "Something for you to think about, you know, when you move to Houston and marry Ronan."

"Slow your roll, sister. Believe me, there are no wedding bells in my near future. I'll be the maid of honor when you marry Brock long before I think about getting married."

"You're probably right. If he asked me today, I would marry him tomorrow."

Alexis looked out the window. "Here comes Anthony."

"You ready?"

"I'm ready." Alexis put down her coffee and waited until the door opened before she said, "If everything goes our way, we should be able to make an offer on the complex in Hollywood and the St. Johns Square project."

"Good morning, ladies," Anthony said when he came into the trailer.

"Good morning, Anthony," Imani said.

"Morning," Alexis said and continued. "I hate that we have to pass on doing Southwark Plaza." Imani nodded. "But I am excited about diversifying our portfolio with St. Johns Square."

"I am too," Imani concurred as Anthony sat down in the chair. "We're looking to make an offer on a one-hundred-unit apartment complex to convert to condos in Hollywood, Anthony."

"You ladies certainly are aggressive," Anthony said.

"We certainly and most assuredly are," Alexis said forcefully.

Imani picked up her Frappuccino. "You want in, Anthony?" she all but sang.

"You know I certainly and most assuredly do," he said as Alexis had. He was excited about the possibility of getting new business, which was what they anticipated. "What's the unit mix?"

"Fifty one-bedroom units, forty two-bedroom units, and ten three-bedroom units," Imani said, hoping that Anthony would feed on her enthusiasm.

Alexis raised both of her hands. "Slow down, roadrunner. I thought we agreed that if we do it, *if*," she repeated passionately, "since both properties are income-producing and low-vacancy, we would allow them to produce some income before we moved forward with converting in Hollywood." She picked up Anthony's revised estimate and held it up. "Especially since we have this unexpected expense in front of us."

"I know, I know. And you're right, Alexis," Imani said, sounding dejected and looking at Anthony. "I need to slow down, and we get this project done first before I go running off to the next one."

Anthony turned quickly to Alexis. "Tell you what, Alexis. You commit to giving me the one-hundred-unit conversion, and I'll give you a ten percent discount on this project. And one more thing I'd like to point out." He pointed to the paper in Alexis's hand. "That is an estimate. The actual cost may be substantially less."

"And it might be substantially more," Alexis said, shaking the paper.

"Come on, Alexis. Give a little," Imani pleaded.

"How would something like that even work?"

"I'm sure the lawyers can work out some promissory language and put it in writing," Imani suggested, and Anthony nodded in agreement.

"At least let me have a look at the specs. Then we can talk about actual numbers."

"I don't have the specs here," Alexis said and cursed herself for not being prepared for the game they were running so well. Imani looked at her sideways. "They're at my office."

"How long would it take you to go get them?" Imani asked.

"I could get them and be back in less than an hour," she promised.

"Why don't you go ahead and do that and bring me back another Frappuccino when you come?"

Alexis stood up. "You want anything, Anthony?"

"Just some coffee."

"I'll be back," Alexis said and left the trailer satisfied that they had Anthony exactly where they wanted him.

As she drove, Alexis was actually surprised by how well their plan was working out. Although it was what they intended, she was amazed by how quickly Anthony jumped on it and went straight to offering them a discount for future business.

When she got to the offices of South Jacksonville Realty, Alexis's intention was to get the specs as quickly as possible and get back to the Plaza. She got out of her car and rushed inside so quickly that she didn't see his car parked in the lot. She spoke to Cynthia as she passed her office and hoped that she wouldn't want to talk about when she was coming back to work. Alexis got to her office, sat down at her desk, and got the file from the drawer.

"Alexis."

She looked up quickly. "Cam? What are you doing here?" she asked, wide-eyed and looking around.

"I needed to talk to you."

Alexis stood up. "Not here. We can talk outside," she said, rushing past him to get out of the office.

Once they were outside and away from the building, Alexis turned quickly to Cameron. "What are you doing here?"

"I haven't heard from you in almost a week. All my calls go straight to voicemail, and you don't respond to my messages. I was worried about you."

Alexis got in his face and pointed. "That doesn't give you the right to just show up here."

Just then, the office door opened. "Is everything all right, Alexis?"

"Everything is fine, Cynthia. Thank you," Alexis said.

After getting a good look at Cameron, Cynthia went back inside.

Alexis shook her head in disgust. "How did you even find me?"

"In case of emergency," Cameron said, and Alexis immediately knew what he was talking about.

Ever since Jelena Grey called her Alexis and not Diamond, the name had been rolling around in his mind. He found himself repeating it over and over.

"Alexis. Alexis. Alexis. Why is that name so familiar to me?" he'd asked himself, and it bothered him until the night before.

He was at Tyriana's house, and when they got finished doing what they were doing, Cameron was lying in bed, and thoughts of the name Alexis returned to him.

"Alexis. Alexis," he had said to himself, and all of a sudden it hit him like a shotgun blast. "Alexis Fox," Cameron had said aloud, and Tyriana punched him in the arm.

"You thinking about some other bitch while you lying in my bed? Nigga, get the fuck out of here!"

Since he was finished doing what he came to do anyway, Cameron got out of Tyriana's bed and left there knowing why the name Alexis was so familiar to him and where he had seen it. It was late, but he drove straight to Hedrick's house. His girlfriend, Paula, still lived there.

"It's late, Cam. What do you want?" she had asked when she opened the door and let him inside.

Cameron gave her a hug and a kiss on the cheek. "I'm sorry to come by so late. But I'm looking for something that Kevin kept."

"It's all right." She rubbed the sleep from her eyes. "What are you looking for?"

"Do you still have that real estate agent's card on the refrigerator door?" he had asked, walking past her on his way to the kitchen.

"No," she had said, following him. "I think I put it in one of the drawers." They rummaged through the

drawers until she said, "Found it." She handed the card
to Cameron.

He had looked at the card. It was Alexis's business card,
and Bells had written "In case of emergency" on it.

"Bells gave this to Kevin years ago. He said that we
should only use it in emergencies."

Over the years, Cameron had looked at that card and
not paid any attention to it each time he'd gone in their
refrigerator.

"The card that Bells gave Hedrick," Alexis said, remembering the day that Bells told her that he had given him
her card.

"Like I said, I hadn't heard from you since Maxwell's
funeral, and I was worried. I didn't know what else to do."

Alexis nodded. "I don't have time to talk now, but meet
me at the condo tonight at eight, and we'll talk then."

"Okay." Cameron nodded. "But you're all right, right?"

"I'm fine, Cam. I just got a lot on my mind and a lot
going on. But we'll talk about that tonight. I gotta go."

Cameron nodded. "Okay. I'll see you tonight."

Alexis watched him walk back to his car and drive away
before she went back inside, got what she came for, left
South Jacksonville Realty, and returned to the Plaza.

Later that evening, once Alexis and Imani had completed their day at the Plaza and had a tentative agreement with Anthony on the condo conversion, she drove
to her condo to wait for Cameron. Since the cat was out
of the proverbial bag, she didn't bother changing into
something appropriate for her Diamond persona. There
was no more need.

"I'm out, Cam. I don't want to do this anymore. So, it's
all yours now." Alexis slid a piece of paper across the
coffee table. "I know that I'm handing you a house in
shambles, but call that number when you're ready to do
business. Ask for Elayah. She's gonna give you a hard

time, but then she'll put you on to a guy named Clarence. I already talked to him. He knows all about you, and he's expecting your call. He promised me that he'll take good care of you."

Cameron sat silent and stunned. He could hardly believe what he was hearing. He knew that she had taken Maxwell's death hard, but that was the last thing he expected her to say.

"Wow," he finally managed. "You serious about this, Diamond?"

"I am. I'm out. It's all yours." Alexis picked up her glass of wine and took a sip. "When Bells died and I stepped in, I never expected to be still doing this all these years later. But now, with the way things are going, I know that it's time for me to move on and do something else."

"I hear you," Cameron said, nodding his head solemnly, but on the inside, he was jumping up and down and screaming, *shit yeah,* at the top of his lungs. Diamond was stepping down, and she had handed the crown to him. Fuck that the house was in shambles. It was his house now. "You sure this is what you wanna do?"

"Yeah, Cam, I'm sure. I thought a lot about it, and I know this is what I wanna do, what I have to do for me right now. I've had my time. I've seen too much." She thought about all the people she had personally killed in the name of business. "And I've done too much, and now I'm done." Alexis raised her glass. "It's your time now, Cam."

Chapter Thirty-four

When Alexis walked out of the building with Cameron, Martel was parked across the street. Because Martel planned to murder Cameron, he had been following him since the day after Maxwell's funeral.

"Alexis?"

He was surprised when he heard about Maxwell, Winder, and the others killed that night. But he was happy because killing Maxwell was next on his list of things to do. It just saved him the trouble of having to do it himself. But there Cameron was with Alexis, and he wondered why.

"What's Cam doing with Alexis?"

His first thought was that pretty-boy Cameron was having sex with Alexis, and that made him mad. Martel had been trying to get with Alexis for years, and she'd turned him down each time. He'd always assumed it was because he was a drug dealer and she looked down on him.

"She acts like she's too good for me, but she'll fuck that pretty nigga."

Martel watched angrily as they stood outside the building and talked for a while before they separated. When he didn't see any indication of a physical relationship when they went their separate ways, Martel figured he was wrong about that. But the question remained. He watched Cameron drive away.

"What's Cam doing with Alexis?" he asked himself again. "Unless Alexis is Diamond."

As Alexis got to her car and got in, Martel had a decision to make. He decided to let Cameron go and follow Alexis. He wasn't surprised when he followed Alexis to her house. He had been there once before with Hareem when Alexis needed some furniture moved. As Alexis pulled into her garage, Martel turned the lights off and parked his car across the street from her house.

He saw the lights come on in the living room, and shortly thereafter, he saw Alexis pass by the curtains and close them. At that point, Martel thought about how long he was going to sit there but decided to wait a while and see if she left the house. If she did leave, he wanted to know where she went.

For Alexis, it had been a long day, but it had been the kind that would define her future. When she returned to the Plaza with the design specs of the hundred-unit apartment complex, she, Imani, and Anthony spent the better part of the day crunching numbers and talking about the feasibility of them moving forward with both projects. Once they had come to a conclusion and reached a tentative agreement about Anthony doing the renovation of the Hollywood property, Imani wanted to see the damages that Anthony had pointed out to Alexis.

"Show me."

For the next hour, the three walked around the building, and he showed Imani examples of rotted framing and pointed out the presence of asbestos, and then Anthony took her to the places throughout the property where there were damaged wires and pipes.

"Like I told Alexis, there is some minor decay damage here and there."

"But that was to be expected," Imani said as they returned to the trailer to talk and finalize their agreement.

After Anthony left, Imani rushed to the nearest liquor store and grabbed a bottle of champagne and returned to the Plaza to celebrate with Alexis. Both ladies felt that the deal that they made with Anthony would be beneficial to all parties and would save them money in construction costs in the future.

"To us." Imani raised a red Solo cup.

"And the future," Alexis toasted, and then she left the Plaza and went to her condo to clear a path to begin that future.

When she arrived at her house, Alexis tossed her keys in the dish by the door and went to sit down on the couch. She had been on her feet all day and was ready to take off those Tims and relax. She sat there for a while, replaying her conversation with Cameron, wondering if she did the right thing but knowing deep in her soul that she did.

I've had my time.

Alexis got up from the couch, and after she poured herself a glass of wine, she grabbed the bottle and headed for the bathroom. She put the bottle down, turned the water on in the tub, and allowed it to fill a little before she dropped a bath bomb in and went to get undressed. After a good soak and a second glass of wine, Alexis dried off and put on a Josie Natori silk-satin caftan and stretched out on her bed. She made herself comfortable, took a deep breath, and then she picked up her cell to call Ronan.

"Hello."

"Can I speak to the sexiest man alive?"

"Hold on, let me see if he can come to the phone." Ronan laughed. "How are you, Alexis?"

"I'm wonderful," she cooed.

"You are." He paused. "What's got you in such a good mood?"

"You, for one."

"You know I like the sound of that."

"But we had a good day today, Imani and I, so we did a little celebrating."

"I can hear it in your voice. How much did you drink?"

"We drank a bottle of champagne, and then I had a private celebration with two glasses of wine in the bathtub. And now I am in bed sipping my third glass and talking to the sexiest man alive. What are you doing?"

"Working on a brief for a client."

Alexis laughed. "I'm having more fun than you are," she teased.

"You most certainly are," Ronan said, thinking that Alexis sounded a little tipsy.

"If you're busy, I can let you go and call you tomorrow."

"No, I would much rather talk to you. I need to take a break from this anyway. Hold on while I pour myself a drink."

"I'll be right here," Alexis said and sipped.

"Okay, I'm back," Ronan said after a while. "Now tell me all about your day and what made you and Imani wanna get drunk and celebrate."

"I'm not drunk."

"I know. I've seen you drunk before. So let's just say you're relaxed." Ronan paused. "So, what's going on in your world?" he asked, and Alexis told him all about the progress at the Plaza, the two deals that they agreed to pursue, and the deal that they made with Anthony. Then he told her about the brief he was writing on whether an agreement constituted the contract between the parties.

"There is one other thing that I'm excited about," Alexis said.

"What's that?"

"I've decided that I'm not going back to South Jacksonville Realty."

"Are you going to work for a different broker?"

"No. I plan to focus on the businesses that I have going. And what I am most excited about is that I plan on spending more time in Houston."

"That's great news. Now I'm excited."

"I am too. I love you, Ronan, and I think we do deserve a real chance to see if it can work between us."

"I do too. All I've been hoping for is another chance."

"I know. And I know it's been me standing in the way of that."

"You just needed time, that's all."

"I've been thinking a lot about my future and what I want it to look like, and I know that I want it to include you. And I realize for that to happen, I have to be the one to make some changes." Alexis paused and thought about telling him everything. "There's a lot that you don't know about me, and I have to put it all behind me in order to have the future that I see for myself. Change. Change is a good thing. It's how we grow," she said, quickly deciding that Ronan never having a reason to know anything about her Diamond life meant that she had truly put it all behind her.

"I have to say that you have just made me the happiest man in the world."

"I'm happy too. Happy when I think about the future," Alexis said, closed her eyes, and imagined a future without drugs. A future where she was just Alexis Fox: entrepreneur and investor.

"I am totally blown away. This was the last thing I expected today."

"Me too. I had no idea we'd be having this conversation when I woke up this morning."

"So, when should I expect all this to happen?"

"Well, you know I still have so much going on here, so I was thinking about buying a condo there and traveling back and forth."

"Oh."

"What?"

"Honestly?"

"Tell me."

He chuckled. "I don't know why, but I had visions of you moving in with me, that's all."

"And I know that I will be spending some time at your house until I buy something. If you want me to, that is."

"Of course I want you to."

"But I think that if we are truly going to start over and give this a chance, I don't think jumping into living together after we've been apart all this time gives us the best chance."

Ronan paused and thought about what she'd said, and it made sense to him. "I agree with you, and you're right, but I got caught up in the idea of your face being the last thing I see every night and the first thing I see every morning."

"Aw. That is so sweet of you to say. I wish I could kiss you right now."

"I wish you could do a lot more than kiss me right now."

Alexis paused to think. "We've got a big day tomorrow, but I will call you and let you know what the next couple of days look like. You never know, I might call you and let you know what time my flight is landing in Houston."

"It would be the perfect end to this conversation. You're already talking about making my dream a reality, and now you're talking about showing up in person to do more than just kiss me. This night couldn't get any better."

"I am looking forward to hearing you say sweet, romantic things like that to me all the time. I really missed that when I ran you off."

"And on that note, I'm going to let you go and get back to this brief. But thank you so much, Alexis, for making my night."

"It was my pleasure, sir."

"I really, really do hope that you make it here so you can make my night tomorrow."

"Good night, Ronan."

"Good night, Alexis. I love you."

"I love you too," Alexis said, and then she ended the call, put her phone down, reached over, and turned off the light.

When Alexis turned off the light in her bedroom, Martel started the car and waited for a while to see if the garage door was going to open. After waiting for five minutes, he dropped the car in drive and drove off without getting an answer to his question. Could Alexis Fox actually be Diamond? And if Alexis actually was Diamond, would it change his plan to kill her?

Martel agreed with Hareem. What he was doing was why they were able to recruit her people. What Martel disagreed about was Hareem's belief that he didn't need to kill anybody else. Once he killed Cameron and then Diamond, they would have it all, and there would be no need to recruit her people. But he was getting ahead of himself.

"First things first."

Chapter Thirty-five

The following day, Martel was back on Cameron, looking for an opportunity to kill him. In the short time that he had been following Cameron, Martel found him to be a creature of habit. There were certain places where he like to eat, certain women—Dawnesha, Viera Stone, and Tyriana—he liked to see, and certain places he liked to meet with his boys. Those were the places Martel would avoid because the numbers were bad for him.

The most logical choice was Dawnesha, the one who worked as a bartender at Chili's. He was guaranteed to be there every night that she worked, at a certain time, and he would be there until closing. That would be the easiest place, but that wouldn't be until later that night, and Martel didn't want to wait that long. At eight o'clock that morning, Martel was parked in a spot where he could see Ollie's Kitchen on Twenty-first Street. He had been there for about an hour when he saw Cameron's Toyota Tundra pull into the parking lot.

Feeling this was as good an opportunity as any, Martel picked up his gun. He figured that he could make it to Cameron before he got out of the car, kill him, and be gone. He was about to get out when he saw more cars that he recognized turning into the parking lot. Martel put down his gun and watched Diamond's men meet up in the parking lot before going inside. It was a couple of hours later when Cameron and who were now his men came out of Ollie's Kitchen and went their separate ways.

Martel started the car and made a bet with himself about where Cameron was going next.

"My money's on Tyriana Kelly."

And sure enough, Martel followed Cameron straight to her apartment. But neither Cameron nor Martel was prepared for what they saw when they got there. On the grass directly below the balcony of Tyriana's third-floor apartment were all of his clothes, shoes, and other things that had been left there as well as the appliances that he had bought for her.

Cameron jumped out of his truck, calling Tyriana at the same time.

"What the fuck you want?"

"What the fuck is wrong with you?" Cameron shouted as he walked around his stuff in the grass.

"What the fuck is you talking about?"

"I'm outside and—"

"Good. Now you can get your shit out from in front of my house. Thinking about some other bitch while you're lying in my bed." Tyriana came out on the balcony. "Go to fuckin' hell, and don't call me no more!" she screamed and threw the phone at Cameron before she went back inside.

Martel laughed as he watched Cameron dodge the phone and then begin picking up items of clothes. He gave some thought to walking up behind him while he was distracted and shooting him point-blank in the back of the head, but there were too many eyes on the show at that point. So, Martel waited, and when Cameron left there, he followed him for the rest of the afternoon.

He knew that his next opportunity was coming when Martel noticed that Cameron was heading for the Cypress Landing apartments on Moncrief Road. That was where Viera Stone lived. When he parked his truck, Cameron was on the phone with Tyriana, trying to explain why he had mentioned Alexis's name, but she wasn't interested in anything that he had to say.

Her last words to him were, "Fuck you!"

Cameron shook his head, put the phone in his pocket, and opened the door.

"What's up, Cam?" Martel said and shot Cameron in the head.

Martel pushed Cameron into the passenger seat and got in the driver's seat. He shot him twice more in the chest and started the truck. He drove the truck away from there, and when he stopped, Martel got out and put Cameron back in the driver's seat. Once he had put the seat belt on, he closed the door and walked away.

Chapter Thirty-six

Alexis woke up that morning on a mission. Whether her schedule permitted it or not, and even if she had to fly back in the morning, she was going to Houston that night. Therefore, when she left the house that morning, her bag was packed and in the trunk.

Her day at the Plaza was a busy one as she followed Anthony around, getting in the way at times, as his men began replacing the rotted framing. She learned a lot of good information not just about how to identify rotted framing, but about how to stay out of the way as well.

It was late in the afternoon when Imani called and said that she was in the trailer. Alexis went to the trailer and told Imani about her plan to go to Houston that night. Anthony got to the trailer shortly after, and after they talked about the day's progress and his expectations for the following day, Alexis was out of there and was able to catch an American Airlines flight that departed Jacksonville at 5:35 p.m., had a layover of an hour and forty-five minutes in Charlotte, and arrived in Houston at 10:32 that night.

While she was there, Alexis turned off her phone so she could relax and enjoy the time with Ronan as they explored the greater Houston area. With her drug queen pin life behind her, Alexis was able to take it easy and take pleasure in it all. Ronan had gone out of his way to gather information about how an out-of-state broker could sell in the state of Texas. Even though she didn't think that she was going to be selling real estate once she made the move, it was good information to have in case she changed her mind.

"You could associate yourself with a Texas broker who would handle all the negotiations and listings," he shared.

"That's not gonna happen."

"Or you would have to obtain a Texas real estate license."

"That's what I thought."

"I looked into something called real estate reciprocity."

"That's just an agreement between states that fast-tracks the process of getting a license in their state. Most times it allows you to skip the prelicense courses and go straight to taking the real estate exam."

While Alexis was there, she also paid particular attention to potential properties that she and Imani might be interested in. One that caught her interest was the Clear Lake Apartment Homes, which was comprised of 240 units. She was so excited about the property that Alexis turned on her phone to call Imani, and that was when she found out that she was in Socotra, a coastal town in northern Yemen, with Brock.

"He said that the sunsets here are beautiful, and he wanted to share it with me, so here we are."

"That is so romantic," Alexis said, and they planned to get together in a few days when each returned to Jacksonville. After that, Alexis turned off her phone again so she could enjoy her time with Ronan uninterrupted.

Since Ronan had meetings in Dallas, it was four days later when Alexis booked a 10:06 a.m. nonstop United flight to Jacksonville, and she was back in the city at 1:26 p.m. Since she had a taste for Jamaican food, she stopped at Caribbean Paradise for jumbo oxtail with rice, cabbage, fried plantains, and an additional side of mac and cheese. When she got home, Alexis aired out the house and ate before she got around to turning her phone on and checking her messages. The first was from Detective Blakey.

"It's Horace. It's very important that you call me as soon as you get this message, Alexis."

The next message was from a Detective LaToyia Chisholm. "This message is for Alexis Fox. Ms. Fox, this is Detective Chisholm with the Jacksonville Sheriff's Office. It's very important that you call me as soon as you get this message."

After checking the rest of her messages, Alexis called Detective Blakey.

"Finally," Blakey said when he answered. "Where have you been?"

"Houston."

"I thought so."

"What's wrong, Horace?"

"We need to talk as soon as you can. How soon can you meet me?"

"I can meet you right away. What's wrong, Horace?"

"Meet me at the usual spot," he said and ended the call.

An hour later, Alexis was standing alone at the rail by the St. Johns River in front of the Hyatt Regency when Detective Blakey came rushing up.

"Sorry to keep you waiting," the out-of-breath detective said.

"It's okay. What's wrong?"

"Cameron is dead. He was murdered four days ago. And you're a person of interest in his murder."

"Me? I wasn't even here. How did I get to be a person of interest?" Alexis asked frantically as she pointed to herself.

"His body was found dead in his truck in a strip mall less than a mile from South Jacksonville Realty."

"Oh, no."

"The police have a statement from somebody who said they saw the two of you arguing outside the office the day before he was murdered."

"Cynthia." She shook her head. "Cynthia saw me and Cam talking, but we weren't arguing."

"What was Cameron doing at your office? I thought he didn't know about your other life."

"He didn't, but he found out. How he found out is a long story, but he found out. He hadn't heard from me in a few days, and he was worried about me." Alexis paused and looked at the detective. He needed to know what she had planned. "I'm out, Horace. That night I told Cam that I was out and he could have it all."

"I'm glad to hear that you finally came to your senses after all these years, but that doesn't change the fact that you're a person of interest in his murder."

"I know."

"I'm going to assume that since you're out and you gave it all to him, you didn't kill him."

"No!" she shouted to proclaim her innocence. "I didn't kill him," she said softer.

"I didn't think so. You need to talk to the police, Alexis."

"I know."

"I think it would look better if you came in voluntarily with me."

"I agree, but not right now. There are some things that I need to do before I talk to the cops." Alexis paused. "What do they have on me, Horace? Do I need to come with a lawyer?"

Or should I catch the first flight out of the country?

"It's not my case, so as far as I know, all they have is the location where they found the body and the witness saying that the two of you argued. Nothing about Diamond. At least not yet."

"Okay. I'll meet you at the zone four sheriff's office substation tomorrow morning at nine o'clock."

"Okay. Until then, you be careful, Alexis."

"I will, and thank you for the heads-up, Horace," she said, walking away.

Alexis walked back to her car and drove away thinking about the words "person of interest" and what that meant to her. More importantly, she wondered what it meant to the cops who were investigating the case. The definition of a person of interest refers to someone who authorities believe to be possibly involved in a crime or might have information pertinent to a crime but has not been charged or arrested. Or it could be someone who can provide information that led the police to a suspect. The other possibility, the one Alexis was concerned about, was that the police considered her a person of interest who might turn into a suspect, although she knew that she couldn't or shouldn't become a suspect in Cameron's murder, simply because she didn't do it.

But we are talking about the police. Alexis was under no delusion that even though she had nothing to do with it, she could be arrested, charged, and convicted of his murder.

But what Alexis was most concerned about, and with good reason, was that the police had connected her to Cameron, but had they connected her to Diamond? She didn't know whether they had, and if Detective Blakey didn't know, she had no way to find out. It was a position that Alexis, the plotting planner, didn't like to be in. The planner in her liked to know and be in control of, if possible, everything she did, said, or had going on around her. She was always very deliberate in her approach, developing a detailed strategy to deal with whatever it was that she had to deal with. Alexis had no control at all of this situation, and that scared her.

When Alexis got to her house, she parked in the garage, left the car running, and went inside. She went straight to her bedroom and sat down on the bed. Alexis opened her nightstand drawer and took out the phone that she used to use to communicate with Cameron. She thought about turning the phone on to see if there was anything in Cameron's messages that would provide her with information on what happened or that may help her deal with the police. But when she considered the possibility that the police might be just waiting for the phone to be turned on so they could track it, Alexis decided against it.

Alexis closed the nightstand drawer and returned quickly to her car and drove out on Roosevelt Boulevard and headed for Green Cove Springs, a city in the county seat of Clay County. The forty-minute ride gave Alexis more time to think about what she was going to do next. The idea of getting on Interstate 10 and driving to Houston crossed her mind. She could be there in twelve hours, but the question was, what then?

Would she involve Ronan in her drama, running the risk that one day the police would knock on the door and arrest her for murder, drug trafficking, and money laundering? Or would Houston just be a stopover to say goodbye to Ronan on her way to Mexico?

"You are seriously tripping," Alexis said aloud as she arrived in Green Cove Springs, and she drove to Spring Park on the western bank of the St. Johns River.

Alexis turned off the car and got out, taking the burner phone with her. She walked to the end of the south dock kayak launch. She took apart the phone, dropped it on the ground, and then began stomping it with her foot as hard as she could until the phone was in pieces. Then she meticulously picked up each piece of the phone and threw it in the St. Johns River.

Even though she had completed her task, Alexis stood there for a while, staring out at the river, thinking about what other physical evidence there was in her possession that could possibly tie her to Cameron. Diamond's Jaguar F-Type coupe, her condo, and everything else she owned were all purchased by a shell company that was buried under several other shell companies. Since there was nothing that could connect Alexis Fox to those shell companies, Alexis wasn't as worried about them. But since, one way or the other, she was finished with the Diamond persona, she would see about liquidating those assets at her first opportunity.

Alexis went back to her car and left Spring Park on her way back home to Jacksonville. On her way back to the city, Alexis began thinking about the police and what they would ask her. Knowing that it depended entirely on what they knew, she tried to think of a way that she could find out what they had. But there was none, not one that she could think of anyway. She would be walking into the sheriff's office totally in the dark.

The question arose again: *do I need to come with my lawyer?*

Alexis pulled into her driveway, thinking that lawyering up might make her seem guilty, but it may be the only thing that ensured that she walked out of the sheriff's office a free woman. Now that she was home, Alexis kicked off her heels, poured herself a glass of wine, and headed for the bathroom. She took a hot bath, and then she got into bed.

"I'll deal with everything else in the morning," she said aloud and turned off the lamp.

Chapter Thirty-seven

The following morning when Alexis woke up, she felt refreshed. Despite her situation, she slept well. She lay there for a while, staring up at the ceiling, wondering if there was anything else that she could do to be ready for the police. She giggled.

"Wearing something that screams I am an innocent real estate agent and not a murderous drug queen pin would be nice," Alexis mused and got out of bed thinking that she needed to choose something extremely conservative, bordering prudish. "What color says I'm innocent?"

With that thought in mind, Alexis selected a white and gold Valentino tie-neck midi dress because the symbolism and color meaning behind white represented innocence, simplicity, purity, and perfection. She completed her innocent look with a pair of Valentino Garavani rock-stud strappy sandals and a small one-stud woven straw shoulder bag. Alexis took a look at herself in the full-length mirror, and satisfied with her look, she grabbed her keys from the dish and headed out.

While she was in the car, she called Detective Blakey to let him know that she was on her way to the sheriff's office. He told Alexis that he would be waiting for her at the Ellianos Coffee that was in the Cedar Hills Shopping Center where the sheriff's office was located, and they would walk there together.

"Sounds good," Alexis said and was about to hang up when she thought of a question. "Horace."

"Yes, Alexis."

"Have you heard anything else?"

"Sorry, Alexis, I haven't. But that is not necessarily a bad thing," Detective Blakey said.

"Okay. I'll see you soon."

When Alexis arrived at the Cedar Hills Shopping Center, she met Detective Blakey at the coffee shop, and after talking strategy over coffee, they walked down to the sheriff's office substation and approached the desk sergeant.

"How can I help you, ma'am?"

"My name is Alexis Fox, and I'm here to see Detective Chisholm," Alexis said with the detective standing by her side.

The desk sergeant looked at Blakey and nodded in acknowledgment of his presence at her side. "Have a seat, and I will let Detective Chisholm know that you are here."

"Thank you," she said, and the detective nodded as they went to sit down.

It was twenty minutes later when an officer came and escorted Alexis to a conference room, and another thirty minutes before the door opened and the detectives came into the room.

"Good morning, Ms. Fox. I'm Detective Chisholm, and this is my partner, Detective Doyle."

"Sorry to keep you waiting." They sat down. "Thank you for coming, Ms. Fox. We just have a few questions for you. We'll try not to keep you for very long," Doyle said.

"Can I get you something to drink?" Chisholm asked.

"No, thank you, I'm fine," Alexis said.

"Good, then let's get started," Chisholm said.

"Ms. Fox," Doyle began, "are you familiar with a gentleman named Thaddeus Cameron?"

Is that his real name? Alexis paused for a moment as if the name weren't familiar to her.

Chisholm slid an image of Cameron in front of her. "This man?"

"Yes, I am familiar with him."

"How would you describe your relationship?" he asked.

Alexis shook her head and smiled. "I wouldn't call it a relationship, but I do know him."

"Tell me about that," Doyle sat back and said.

"I met him . . . about a month ago, I guess. He was in line behind me at Starbucks. We talked briefly. I told him that I was a real estate agent, and he said that he was interested in buying a house, and I gave him my card. That was the end of that, until he came to my office one day last week." Alexis leaned forward and raised one finger in the air to emphasize her point. "Not to buy a house, mind you, but to ask me to go out with him."

"So you met Mr. Cameron at a Starbucks, you gave him your card, and sometime later, he showed up at your office and asked you to go out with him. What happened then, Ms. Fox?" Doyle asked.

"I escorted him out of the office."

"What happened after you escorted him out?"

"When we got outside, I told him how inappropriate that was. He said that he was just trying to ask me out. And I told him that didn't give him the right to just show up there," Alexis said, leaning forward and pointing at the detectives as she said each word.

"Just like that?" Chisholm asked.

"Excuse me?"

"Were you pointing in his face just like that?"

Alexis smiled. "Yes." She chuckled and folded her hands in front of her. "I have a tendency to talk with my hands."

Doyle glanced at Chisholm. "You escort him out, you tell him that it's not cool just showing up at your place of business like that. What happened then, Ms. Fox?" he asked.

"He apologized and then he left."

Doyle leaned forward quickly. "He didn't give you any argument?"

"No," Alexis said calmly. "He said he was sorry to have bothered me, he left, and I went back inside."

"And you hadn't heard from him since?" Doyle asked.

"No, sir. I haven't."

"You mind if I have a look at your phone?"

"Not at all." Alexis unlocked her phone and handed it to Doyle.

"Thank you, Ms. Fox," he said and glanced at his partner.

Chisholm smiled. "Where you been, Ms. Fox? I called and left you a message days ago. What took you so long to call me back?"

"I've been in Houston the past four days, and my phone was off while I was there."

"Why was your phone off?" Chisholm asked.

Alexis smiled. "I have a friend there. Well, he's more than just a friend. Anyway, I turned off my phone because I'm thinking about moving to Houston to give our relationship a second chance, and I wanted to spend that time with him and not be distracted with business."

"Good luck. I hope it works out," Chisholm said.

"Thank you. I hope it does too."

"When did you get back to Jacksonville?" she asked.

"Yesterday afternoon."

"Why didn't you call me then?"

"I didn't turn my phone on until later in the evening."

"Thank you, Ms. Fox," she said and glanced at her partner.

"Ms. Fox, you said that you've been in Houston for the past few days."

"That's right."

"When did you leave?"

"Thursday."

"Tell me about that day, Ms. Fox."

"I went to work that morning, my business partner, Imani Mosley, and I recently bought the Plaza Hotel, and we're in the process of renovating it."

"Congratulations."

"Thank you."

"Were you there all day?" Doyle asked.

"Yes."

"What time did you leave?"

"Oh, let's see." She paused and rubbed her chin. "Imani got there about two, two thirty, we had a meeting with our general contractor, Anthony Tortora, so I'm thinking it was sometime around four, maybe a little after. Then I went to the airport and caught the flight to Houston."

"What time was your flight, do you remember?" Doyle asked.

"It was an American Airlines flight that left about five thirty."

"Thank you, Ms. Fox," Doyle said.

"Would you mind telling me what this is all about?"

"Thaddeus Cameron was murdered the day after your interaction with him."

"Oh, my God," Alexis said, covering her mouth and doing her best to look horrified by the news. "That's terrible."

And then slowly, her facial expression changed, and she dropped her head a little. When Alexis raised her head, her eyes were wide open, and a panicked look covered her face.

"Do you think I killed him?" Alexis sat straight up. "Do I need a lawyer?"

"No, Ms. Fox. Calm down. Nobody is accusing you of anything," Chisholm said. "These are just preliminary questions."

"We're just gathering information. That's all we're doing here today." Doyle glanced at his partner. "Can I speak with you for a second, Detective?" He stood up. "Would you excuse us for a second, Ms. Fox?"

Alexis nodded, but she said nothing. However, she was glad that it seemed to be over, and the name "Diamond" never came up.

Detective Chisholm stood up, and they left the conference room.

"What do you think?" Doyle asked when they got into the hallway.

"I don't like her for it. I mean, look at her." The detectives looked at Alexis through the conference room window while they talked. "A minute ago, she was all poise and personality. Now look at her." The detectives discreetly glanced at Alexis fidgeting nervously in her chair. "She's a nervous wreck."

"I don't like her for it either. She doesn't seem like the type. And on top of that, the timing is wrong. There's no way she could have left the hotel, driven to Orange Park, killed him, and made it back to the airport in time to catch a five thirty flight."

"I agree. I believe it went exactly the way she said. She met the guy, and he arrogantly just showed up at her job," Chisholm said. "And if that's the case, where's her motive?"

"But what's biting my ass is where the killer dumped the body. It's clear from the blood in the passenger seat that the body was moved and then driven to that mall. But why? To set her up, maybe?"

"Or there may be some other significance to where the truck was dropped that may have nothing to do with her."

"Coincidence?"

Chisholm chuckled. "I know that is a curse word to you."

"That's because there is no such thing as a coincidence. Shit gets done for a reason." He took a deep breath. "Okay, let's check out her alibi, talk to the contractor and her partner, and check with the airline to see what time she actually checked in."

"Okay," Chisholm said and started to go back into the conference room.

"But I think that we need to put a car on her for a couple of days. It may be something, it may be nothing, but I can't get past the killer dropping the truck near her job." He shook his head. "I think there's more to this." He reached for the conference door handle. "Whether Miss Poise and Personality knows there's more to it or not."

When the detectives went back into the conference room, Alexis sat up straight and folded her hands in front of her.

"That's all the questions that we have for now," Doyle said. "You're free to go."

"If we have any more questions for you, we'll be in touch," Chisholm said, and Alexis stood up and was escorted out of the conference room.

When they got into the lobby, Alexis picked up her pace and headed toward the spot where Detective Blakey was waiting for her. She all but rushed into his arms and buried her head in his chest, and he comforted her like a father would his daughter.

"How'd it go?"

Alexis turned quickly and pointed to Doyle and Chisholm. "They think I killed somebody!"

"They're just asking questions. Trying to get the facts," he said, patting her on the back as the detectives looked on.

Alexis broke their embrace and shook her head. "But I didn't kill anybody!" she said loud enough for Doyle and Chisholm to hear.

"Then you have nothing to worry about." He started walking her toward the door. "You go on home now, and I will call you if I hear anything."

Alexis nodded hard. "Okay. Thank you for coming with me," she said and left the substation.

When she did, Chisholm walked up to him. "Horace." She nodded respectfully.

"LaToyia." He nodded in recognition.

She motioned with her head as Alexis left the building. "You know her?"

"I do."

"What can you tell me about her?" Chisholm asked.

"I met Alexis years ago. I was the one who had to tell her that her man was killed in jail." He paused to allow that to sink in. "She's a good kid. I call and check on her every once in a while."

"Sarge says she came in with you."

"That's right. She called me last night, panicked, after she got your message."

"What did you tell her?"

"I told her not to worry and told her I'd come in with her."

"You didn't tell her what it was about?"

"No, LaToyia, I didn't. I don't know if she killed this asshole. That's for you to find out. But I thought you deserved to look her in the eye and judge for yourself. So, what does your gut tell you?"

"I don't like her for it. Timeline doesn't work, and I'm not seeing a motive." Chisholm paused. "Doyle's feeling some kind of way about where the truck was dropped, but without more to go on, I am willing to accept that is a coincidence."

"And your partner doesn't believe in coincidences."

"He does not."

Blakey patted Chisholm on the back. "Well, LaToyia, I guess that is where good old-fashioned police work comes in."

She chuckled. "Thanks, old man."

"Anytime."

Chapter Thirty-eight

It had been a few days since Alexis was interviewed by Detectives Doyle and Chisholm, and in that time, she returned to her routine as if she were not a person of interest in Cameron's murder. Therefore, her morning ritual hadn't changed much, but there were a few differences. She still woke up around the same time, but since she was her own boss and wasn't punching a clock, Alexis did allow herself to lie in bed instead of jumping up and rushing. Where she would normally lay out her outfit for the day and take a shower, Alexis took a bath and relaxed.

Once she had dried off, Alexis dressed in jeans, women's Timberland boots, and a hard hat, and headed for the Plaza Hotel and Suites. She knew without having to be told that there was a plainclothes officer following her, so she played it straight down the line. Straight to the Plaza and straight home at night.

"She's boring as hell," Officer Allen said to Doyle after following her for a couple of days. "Straight to work, straight home. Thirty minutes after she gets there, the Grubhub order arrives. And it's lights out at about the same time every night. Boring! Boring as hell. But you know what? I am loving this overtime, so I ain't saying nothing."

"I know it's a boring gig, but stay on her for another couple of days."

"You know you got it," Allen said and went away happy. As for Doyle, he was slowly coming around to agreeing with his partner. "Coincidence."

In addition to having Officer Allen following Alexis, he had subpoenaed her phone records for both her cell phone and office extension, checked her social media presence, and could find no connection between her and Cameron. He had interviewed Anthony Tortora as well as several of his employees, and they each were able to verify that Alexis left the Plaza sometime around four o'clock.

He was able to verify what time she checked in for her flight to Houston. All that remained was to talk to Imani, who hadn't returned from Yemen, but at that point, interviewing her was just him being thorough and covering all of his bases. Once he spoke to her, he would be comfortable with saying that Alexis was no longer a person of interest in Cameron's murder. Therefore, the detectives moved on to canvassing the store owners where the truck was dropped to determine if there were some other reason because, here again, the detective didn't believe in coincidences.

As for Alexis, she was enjoying this time immersing herself in her work and not having to live Diamond's double life. It gave her the opportunity to do more research about properties, both in Texas and Florida, that she would share with Imani when she got back. And spending more time talking on the phone with Ronan was making her feel more comfortable with the direction she was going.

It was settled. Alexis was moving to Houston. Her increased comfort level with Ronan made her more comfortable with him coming to Jacksonville to visit, where, while things were kind of hectic, she went out of her way to avoid any discussion of him coming there.

Another upside to the change in her perspective was it allowed Alexis to see her reality in new ways and that made her feel freer with Ronan. With her Diamond life in her rearview, Alexis no longer felt like she had to hold back pieces of herself. She felt free to express herself, all of her, in ways that she had not allowed herself to in years. And that manifested itself in ways that Ronan found a great deal of pleasure in.

"Damn," was all Ronan could breathe out when he rolled off of her.

But Alexis wasn't finished with him. She sat up in the bed and took him into her mouth, teased his head with her tongue, and then slowly worked her way down. Her lips and tongue were soft and wet. As he began to get harder, she relaxed the muscles in her throat so she could take more of him into her mouth.

Once he was hard again, she straddled his body, lowered herself onto him, and slowly began to move her hips from side to side. Her head drifted back with her mouth open and eyes wide. He kept pushing it to her until she collapsed on his chest, but she didn't stop moving.

"Yeah," she said.

Letting go of her dark past wasn't going to be easy, but Alexis had accepted who and what she was and was trying to move forward. Even if she wanted to, she knew that she couldn't undo her past, but she was finding ways to find peace with it.

"I hate to leave," Ronan said and kissed Alexis.

"I hate for you to leave. But I'll see you soon."

"Not soon enough," he said and took his luggage from the trunk. "I just hate that I couldn't stay another day so I could see Imani."

"I know, but it couldn't be helped. Their flight out of Qatar was delayed, so they missed their connection. She was looking forward to seeing you."

Then there was silence as Alexis and Ronan stared into each other's eyes. She gave him a quick kiss on the cheek. "Go. Call me when you get home."

He picked up his bag. "I will," he said, and Alexis watched Ronan walk into the terminal before she got back in her car and left the airport. She was on her way home when Alexis got a call that she wasn't expecting.

"Hey, lady. You still stuck in Europe?"

"No. We're home," Imani said.

"Home?"

"I got tired of the delays, cancellations, and the hassle, so we chartered a jet and flew home."

"Baller."

"Whatever. So what's been going on?"

"You just missed Ronan for one."

"Although that is important, I was talking more about what was going on with our business."

"I'm driving, so why don't I just stop by and I can tell you everything when I get there?"

"See you when you get here," Imani said, and she ended the call.

When Alexis got to the house, Imani let her in, and they talked in her office. Once Alexis had told Imani what was going on at the Plaza and shared Anthony's daily reports with her, she dropped it.

"Arrested?"

"Well," Alexis giggled, "not arrested, but I was questioned by the police about a murder."

"Murder!"

"Yes, you believe that? A murder."

"Who'd you kill?" Imani asked playfully.

"Some guy I met a couple of weeks ago. He was in line behind me at Starbucks. When I told him that I was a real estate agent and he said that he was interested in buying a house, I gave him my card. But then he showed up at my office and asked me to go out with him."

"And you killed him for that?" Imani asked and shook her finger at Alexis. "You're a bad girl."

"No, I'm not. Not even close. But apparently he was murdered the next day, and get this."

"What?"

"I told him that it wasn't cool for him to just show up like that, and I kindly escorted him out of the office. So we're talking outside, and Miss Cynthia comes out to check on me."

"I heard my woman's name invoked," Hareem said when he came into the room. "What did she do now?"

"Hey, Hareem," Alexis said. "Nothing but tell the police that I was arguing with some thug who got himself killed the next day."

"The police questioned her about the murder," Imani said.

"Do you believe that? Questioning me about a murder?" Alexis asked innocently.

"No," Imani said flatly.

"No, Alexis, I can't see the police questioning you about a murder." Hareem laughed.

"See what I'm saying?" Alexis said as Kimberly came into Imani's office.

"Excuse me, Hareem."

"Yes, Kimberly?"

"Martel is waiting for you in the great room."

"Thank you, Kimberly. Good to see you, Alexis." He chuckled on his way to the door. "And try to stay out of trouble."

"I leave all the trouble to you," Alexis mused as he left the room.

Hareem walked down the hallway to the great room, wondering if it was possible that Alexis was talking about Cameron's murder. Even though Martel hadn't mentioned anything about it, he knew that Martel killed him. Cynthia had told him about the man who came to see Alexis and that she was so worried that she went out to check on her. Hareem never imagined that the man she was talking about was Cameron.

"What's up, baby boy?" Martel said when Hareem came into the great room.

"Marty-mar, what's up?" Hareem sat down next to him. "Did you kill Cameron?"

"Yeah, why?" Martel asked like it was no big deal.

"Why didn't you tell me?"

"I didn't know I had to."

"Would have been good to know."

Martel chuckled. "I kinda did."

"Kinda did what?"

"Tell you. I mean, I didn't come right out and say it, but I did say that now that Cameron is dead, the rest of Diamond's people are falling in line."

Hareem stood up and walked to the window. "There's nobody left, is there?"

"I ain't seen or heard from LaLa, and Diamond must have some soldiers who are still loyal to her, but for the most part, everybody who was making real paper is with us now. The city is ours, just like we planned it the day you dragged my ass up here. You remember? We were rolling down 95 on the way here, and you said, 'Fuck Miami. This the promised land for us.'"

"I remember. The city was wide open, and now it's ours." Hareem turned around. "Ours, Marty-mar, just like I said it would be," Hareem said as he heard Imani's and Alexis's voices coming down the hall. They were passing by the door when Martel saw them.

"Hello, Alexis! Hello, Imani!" Martel shouted from the couch as they passed the room, and they came back to the door.

Alexis stood there staring at Martel and feeling nothing but rage. She knew Martel had either killed her people or ordered their deaths. And now he was sitting there, triumphantly staring her down.

"How you doing, Martel?" Imani asked.

"I'm doing wonderful. Everything in my world is wonderful. What about you, Alexis? How you doing?"

Alexis smiled because, in reality, she should be thanking him. "I am on top of the world, Martel. Things in my world couldn't be any better." She fist-bumped Imani while she continued to stare into his eyes. Had it not been for Martel, she may not have made the choice to get out. "Ain't that right, Imani?"

"And it only gets better from here. Good to see you, guys," Imani said and left the great room with Alexis.

Hareem shook his head and exhaled. "Goddamn, Alexis is so fuckin' fine," he said and plopped down on the couch next to Martel.

"Alexis is Diamond."

"What you talking about? This part of your Alexis fantasy or something?"

"No, Alexis is Diamond."

"No, she's not." Knowing how badly he had always wanted to fuck Alexis, Hareem laughed, but Martel didn't. "You saying fine-ass, 'can't break a fingernail' Alexis is Diamond?"

"That's what I'm saying."

"Stop fuckin' around."

"I'm not. That bitch is Diamond."

"You're crazy. Ain't no way Alexis could be Diamond and Imani not know about it and she not tell me."

"Okay."

It didn't matter whether Hareem believed him. In fact, it really didn't matter whether she was Diamond. It was over, the city was theirs, and that was all that mattered. And besides, if Alexis was Diamond, the police would be all over her soon enough. He looked at Hareem and thought that telling him was a mistake. He stood up.

"I'm out."

"I am too." Hareem stood up. "I gotta run down to the port to handle something."

"You need me to come with you?" Martel asked because he wanted to be in on port activities.

"No. I'll holla at you tomorrow," Hareem said, and they both left the great room on their way to the door.

When they got outside, he looked at Alexis standing by her car talking to Imani, and it occurred to Martel that whether Alexis was Diamond or not, he knew that Diamond would be coming after him for killing Cameron. And if Diamond really was Alexis, she would come after him for leading the police to her. They shook hands, and then Martel watched Hareem get in his Dodge Charger Hellcat and speed away, knowing that he had to kill Alexis.

"But I'm gonna fuck her first."

Chapter Thirty-nine

After agreeing that they would make an offer on the apartment complex in Hollywood, Florida, Alexis said good night to Imani and got in her car. She was thinking about Martel and how the way he looked at her always made her flesh crawl. Alexis shook it off and tried to focus on planning the day that she was going to have the next day. Her plan for the night was to pick up takeout on the way home, eat, take a bath, and have phone sex with Ronan.

"What do you have a taste for?" she asked herself aloud as she drove. When she got to a red light, Alexis unlocked her phone, scrolled through her contacts, and dialed a number.

"Thai Blossom Bistro, how can I help you?"

"I want to place an order to pick up, please."

"Go ahead with your order."

"I want the grilled salmon in panang curry. And can I get that without the pineapples?"

"Grilled salmon in panang curry, no pineapples. Anything else?"

"No, that's it."

"Your name?"

"Fox."

"Be ready in fifteen minutes."

"Thank you," Alexis said, and since Thai Blossom Bistro was on Atlantic Boulevard and it was in the opposite direction, she made a U-turn and headed that way.

However, when she looked in her rearview mirror, Alexis saw that another car had made a U-turn as well. She sped up, and when they didn't speed up to keep pace with her, Alexis thought that she was just being paranoid.

Alexis knew that the reason for her paranoia was Diamond and vowed that part of the following day would be devoted to making moves toward getting out. That meant selling the Jaguar and the condo, and she would donate her clothes and furniture to Goodwill.

She pulled into the parking lot at Thai Blossom Bistro, shut off the car, and got out. Alexis was walking to the restaurant when, out of the corner of her eye, she saw a car pull into the parking lot and park in the back row.

"That's Martel's car," Alexis said and walked a little faster, thinking again that she was being paranoid. Maybe Martel was going someplace in the shopping center, but her instincts told her differently. Alexis went inside the restaurant, and when she got to the counter, she kept going.

"You can't go back there," the girl at the counter said as Alexis went into the kitchen.

"You're not supposed to be back here," the cook said. "Sheila, call the cops," he yelled as Alexis kept going through the kitchen and went out the back door.

Once she was outside, she looked around to get her bearings and see which way to get out of there. Alexis made her way around the building to the front. She looked around the parking lot, and when she didn't see Martel, she started walking back to her car, thinking once again that she was just paranoid when she saw Martel coming out of Thai Blossom Bistro.

When their eyes met, Alexis panicked and started running to her car. Martel started running and was able to make it to the car at the same time that Alexis did. He put his gun in her back.

"Get in."

Alexis opened the door and got in. Martel got in the back seat and put the gun to her head.

"What are you doing, Martel?"

"Shut up, Diamond, and start the car!" Martel shouted.

Alexis started the car, panicked because he knew that she was Diamond, and started thinking about how she was going to get out of this. "Diamond? Who's Diamond?"

Martel hit her hard in the back of the head.

"Ouch! Shit!"

"You're Diamond. Now shut up and drive."

"Where are we going?"

"Shut up and drive out Atlantic, Diamond."

Alexis did as she was told and drove out on Atlantic Boulevard, regretting the decision that she had made years ago not to carry a gun in her Alexis persona. Real estate agent and investor Alexis Fox never needed one until now, and she never believed that anybody would find out that she was Diamond. She looked at Martel in the rearview mirror and wondered how he found out.

"Cam," she said softly. *He was probably following Cam, and that's how he found me.*

Now Alexis wondered how long Martel had been following her, how much he knew, and who he told.

"Make this left here," Martel ordered, and Alexis turned onto Mayport Road.

"Where are we going?"

"Shut up and drive, Diamond."

"No. I will not shut up. I am not Diamond, and you need to tell me where we're going."

"Stop lying. I followed Cameron to that apartment you keep in San Marco," Martel said, and Alexis said nothing. "Yeah, you're Diamond."

"You don't have to kill me. I'm out. Before you killed him, I gave everything to Cameron. I'm moving to Houston."

"Houston?" Martel laughed. "What's in Houston?"

"Nothing," she lied. "Just someplace different that I can start over, go legit."

"That sounds really nice. It does." He pushed the gun against her head. "Too bad it ain't gonna happen. Now slow down and make this next left."

Alexis slowed down and made the left turn into a subdivision as she was told. She had driven past one house with a leasing center sign out front and then saw that the rest of the houses were still under construction.

"Drive to the back," Martel ordered, and Alexis drove slowly past frame house after frame house until they were coming up to a dead end. "Turn right here and go to the house at the end of the street."

"You don't have to kill me, Martel."

"Yes, I do," he said as Alexis slowed down and stopped in front of the last frame house on the street. "Get out."

Martel walked Alexis to the house, holding on to the back of her blouse with his gun pointed at the back of her head. There were no doors on the house, so they walked right in. There was no power in the house, but the streetlight shining through the windows lit up the house. Once they were inside, Martel pushed Alexis to the ground. She began crawling away.

"Please, Martel, you don't have to do this," Alexis pleaded. "I can give you money. Just don't kill me."

Martel stood over her, smiling. "I'm not gonna kill your fine ass yet. We got things to take care of first."

"Police. Freeze!" Officer Allen shouted.

He had been following Alexis since he was assigned to the detail by Detective Doyle. He was in the parking lot when Martel ran down and took Alexis at gunpoint. What was once easy overtime had just gotten serious. Once he saw Martel force Alexis into her car, he called Doyle to report, and then he followed them. When he got to the house, he called for backup and went in after them.

Martel turned quickly and fired at the officer, and Allen fired back. The shot hit Martel in the left shoulder. He stumbled back against the wall from the impact. He looked at Allen. He was lying on the floor, not moving.

Thinking this was her chance to get away, Alexis got to her feet and started to run, but she didn't get far before Martel was on her. He grabbed Alexis, spun her around, and punched her in the face. She hit the ground hard. Martel walked over to Allen's body and kicked the gun away from him.

Alexis shook it off. Her jaw hurt like hell, but she got to her feet and tried to run again.

"No you don't," Martel said and grabbed Alexis before she made it to the door.

He reached back and punched Alexis in the face again, and she dropped to the floor like a rock. When she opened her eyes, the room seemed as if it were spinning, but she could see Martel coming toward her. Alexis started crawling backward to get away when she felt Officer Allen's gun. She picked it up, pointed it at Martel, and pulled the trigger. The shot hit Martel in the chest, but he kept coming toward her. Alexis fired again. Martel stopped in his tracks, his knees buckled, and he went down face-first.

Alexis let the gun slip from her hand and stretched out on the floor, glad to be alive. She lay there, trying to catch her breath and compose herself, but she knew that she had to get outta there. Alexis picked up the gun and wiped her fingerprints off, and then she put it back in the cop's hand. She stood up and was about to make her way to the door when Alexis saw a Jacksonville Sheriff's Office cruiser pull up outside, and two cops got out.

They shined their flashlights at Officer Allen's car, and not seeing him in there, the cops drew their weapons and moved quickly toward the house.

"Shit," Alexis said and thought about how she was going to explain being in a vacant house with a dead cop and a dead drug dealer. She got back down on the floor in the spot where Martel hit her and closed her eyes just before the police came in.

"Police!" they shouted when they entered.

"I got bodies," one said. "Clear the rest of the house," he said and went to Officer Allen's body. He took his pulse. "He's dead." He stood up and moved toward Alexis.

"The house is clear," the other cop said.

The cop checked Alexis for a pulse. "She's alive."

"He's not," the other said after checking for a pulse on Martel. "I'll call it in," he said and walked outside.

"Ma'am." He shook her lightly. "Ma'am, are you all right?"

Suddenly Alexis bounced up, swinging at the cops. "Don't hurt me!" she screamed, and the cop grabbed and smothered her in his arms.

"Ma'am, ma'am, I'm a cop. You're all right," he kept repeating and held her until Alexis stopped hitting him and calmed down. "You're all right."

Chapter Forty

"Can you tell me what happened, Ms. Fox?" Detective Chisholm asked.

Once Alexis had calmed down, she was taken to the emergency room at the Mayo Clinic to be examined, and they treated her wounds. Her lower lip was busted, she had a black eye, and her jaw was swollen, but she was going to be fine. Once the doctors took care of the minor cuts and bruises and gave her a cold compress for the swelling in her face, Alexis was admitted and taken to a room for observation. It was midafternoon when Detectives Doyle and Chisholm arrived in the room to question Alexis about what had happened the night before.

"Take your time, Ms. Fox," Doyle added. Once he got the call from Officer Allen that Alexis had been taken at gunpoint, he had called Chisholm, and they arrived at the murder scene shortly after the ambulance arrived.

"I was going to pick up some takeout when Martel came up behind me with a gun and forced me to drive to that house. He hit me a few times, and that's all I remember."

"You sure know how to pick them, Ms. Fox. Notorious drug dealers, I mean," Chisholm began. "First Thaddeus Cameron was murdered the day after he tried to date you, and now Martel. So, how do you know Martel?" Chisholm leaned forward. "Or did you meet him at a Starbucks too?"

"No, ma'am. I've known Martel for five years. He is a close friend of my business partner's brother." Alexis hated that she had to involve Imani in this, but she had no choice.

"Imani Mosley." Chisholm glanced at Doyle.

"And her brother would be Hareem Mosley?" Doyle clarified.

"Yes."

Chisolm leaned close to Doyle. "Another known drug dealer."

"Tell me about your relationship with Martel Gresham, Ms. Fox," Doyle said, ignoring her comment, but it was true—Alexis did seem to know a lot of people involved in the drug game. It made him curious about her potential involvement. But he had checked her out, and as far as he could tell, Alexis Fox was not involved in the game. However, Chisholm wasn't convinced.

"Where there's smoke there's usually fire," was what she'd told her partner, but to this point, she hadn't found anything either.

"He repulses me," Alexis began. "He has been asking me . . . to go out with him in the most vulgar and disgusting ways possible practically from the day we met."

"How did you meet the Mosleys?" Doyle asked.

"I sold them their house."

"I see," Chisholm said.

"Tell us about that night, Ms. Fox."

"I went to Imani's house. She had just gotten back from her trip, and I went by there to update her on the goings-on while she was gone. Martel was at the house when I was getting ready to leave. We had our usual tense exchange, and I left. But I was still outside when he came out with Hareem. When I left the house, I guess he followed me."

"How do you know he followed you?"

"I didn't know for sure. I was on A1A on my way home when I decided to stop at Thai Blossom Bistro, to get some grilled salmon in panang curry, and I made a U-turn, and I saw a car make a U-turn too."

"How did you know it was Martel following you?"

"I didn't know it was him. I just saw a car make a U-turn."

"Did you call the police?" Chisholm asked.

"No."

"Why not? You see that a car is following you. Why don't you call the police?" Chisholm asked again.

"Because after a while I didn't see anybody behind me, so I honestly thought that I was just being paranoid."

"Go on, Ms. Fox. When did you first realize that Mr. Gresham was indeed following you?" Chisholm asked.

"When I got to the restaurant, I saw his car pull into the parking lot." Alexis paused and looked at Doyle because he seemed to be more sympathetic to her story. "I know his car, but even then, I thought maybe he was going to another store in the same plaza."

Doyle sat back. "Coincidence," he said in disgust and glanced at Chisholm.

"When did you realize that it wasn't a coincidence?" she asked.

"When he ran me down and forced me to drive to that house!" Alexis said with attitude. "I'm sorry."

"That's all right, Ms. Fox," Doyle said, and Chisholm rolled her eyes.

"What happened when you got to the house?" she asked.

"All I remember is him hitting me."

"I see." Chisholm rolled her eyes. "What do you think was going to happen?"

"I think that he was going to rape and kill me."

"Did he say that?" Chisholm asked, and Doyle looked strangely at his partner.

"No, Detective Chisholm, he didn't."

"Then what made you think that he was going to rape and kill you?"

Alexis glanced at Doyle and then turned to Chisholm and rolled her eyes. *You know what? I'm tired of your shit, bitch.* She pointed in her face.

"Because he's been asking to fuck me in the most vulgar and disgusting ways since the day that I had the extreme displeasure of meeting him. And then last night, he dragged me to an empty house at gunpoint. That's what made me think that Martel was going to rape and then kill me, Detective Chisholm."

Doyle shook his head, covered his mouth, and chuckled. "I think that we have all that we need, Ms. Fox," he said, seeing that this was quickly developing into a catfight between the two ladies, but he had a good idea where it was coming from.

Detective Chisholm sucked her teeth and stood up. "If we have any more questions for you, Ms. Fox, we'll be in touch," she said and all but stormed out of the room.

Once again, Doyle shook his head. "Thank you, Ms. Fox. You get some rest and heal." He walked to the door, stopped, and turned to face Alexis. "I am sorry that this happened to you," he said and went out into the hallway where Chisholm was waiting.

"'I'm sorry this happened to you,'" she said mockingly as they walked away from Alexis's room. "I know you're not falling for her bullshit, are you?"

"What bullshit?"

"What bullshit? Come on, Jack. Can't you see that there is something else going on with her and these guys? Or are you just blinded by her pretty face?"

No, it's those amazing fucking legs and those nice-sized tits she's hiding behind those loose clothes she wears, he thought. "You're not jealous, are you?"

"Of what? Her? Please. You know me better than that."

"I do, and that's why I asked."

"What's that supposed to mean?"

That you have a problem with female suspects, especially if they're pretty, and Alexis Fox is drop-dead fucking gorgeous, he thought but thought better of saying. "That there's nothing there," he said instead.

"There is something else to her. You just don't want to see it."

"Look, I thought there was more to it too. But where's the evidence that there's more?"

Chisolm said nothing.

"That's what I thought. There's nothing there."

"I know. It's just a feeling, and I get it every time her mouth opens and words come out."

"Well, I trust your instincts. So, if you think she's more involved than she appears to be, stay on her and prove it."

"I am."

"This time, try doing it without getting accused of harassing her," Doyle said as they left the hospital. The last time that Chisholm had one of those feelings, she stayed on the woman until she filed a complaint against the detective for harassment.

"Never gonna let me live that down, are you?"

"Nope."

"Let's go talk to the Mosleys. See if they back up her story," Chisolm said, and the detectives got in their car.

When the detectives left the room, Alexis knew that she was going to have a problem with Chisolm. She had met women like the detective before. She was a dog with a bone, and she would not let this go. Therefore, Alexis knew that once she got out of the hospital, she would need to make sure that there was nothing more that the detective could find that tied her to Cameron, Martel, or Diamond for that matter.

Alexis understood that a lot of that, and eventually her freedom, might depend entirely on what Imani told the police when they interviewed her. Although it was the truth and they had discussed her revulsion for Martel many times, she needed her to confirm it for the detectives.

And then there was Hareem she had to be worried about. Did Martel tell Hareem that she was Diamond? And if he did, did Hareem tell Imani?

She needed to be the one to tell her.

But how do you tell your best friend that you've been lying to her for years? Alexis didn't know, and she knew that it was a conversation that they needed to have. All she could do was hope that it wouldn't affect their business relationships and that their personal relationship would survive.

It was early that same evening when Imani tapped gently on her hospital room door. "Hi," she said, smiling, and waved.

"Hi." Alexis waved back.

"Can we come in?"

"Of course you can," Alexis said, and Imani came into the room with Brock.

"How are you feeling, Alexis?"

"I feel like I got my ass kicked."

"That's because you got your ass kicked," Brock said, and he sat down. Imani came to the bed and sat down.

"Thanks for pointing that out, Brock," Alexis said.

"Well, girlfriend, you have looked better," Imani said.

"I know, and I've felt better, believe me."

"What happened?" Imani asked, and Alexis told the story of how Martel followed and then kidnapped her.

"Well, I talked to the police." Imani paused. "That female detective—"

"Chisholm."

"She's a real piece of work."

"Yeah, she's a little special."

"She is, but I told her about how Martel treated you."

"Thank you. What did she say?"

"She acted like she didn't believe me at first. Like you had something going on with Martel and I was just covering it up for you. But after going around and around a couple of times, she finally said okay."

"Did she talk to Hareem?"

"No, he wasn't there when they came." Imani paused. "You know what I don't understand?"

"What's that?"

"How did you know Cameron anyway?" Imani asked.

"Because she's Diamond," Brock said, and Imani's jaw dropped.